CHRISTMAS CASTLES

SOUL SISTERS AT CEDAR MOUNTAIN LODGE, BOOK 10

JUDITH KEIM

PRAISE FOR JUDITH KEIM'S NOVELS

THE BEACH HOUSE HOTEL SERIES

"Love the characters in this series. This series was my first introduction to Judith Keim. She is now one of my favorites. Looking forward to reading more of her books."

BREAKFAST AT THE BEACH HOUSE HOTEL *is an easy, delightful read that offers romance, family relationships, and strong women learning to be stronger. Real life situations filter through the pages. Enjoy!"*

LUNCH AT THE BEACH HOUSE HOTEL *– "This series is such a joy to read. You feel you are actually living with them. Can't wait to read the latest one."*

DINNER AT THE BEACH HOUSE HOTEL *– "A Terrific Read! As usual, Judith Keim did it again. Enjoyed immensely. Continue writing such pleasantly reading books for all of us readers."*

CHRISTMAS AT THE BEACH HOUSE HOTEL *– "Not Just Another Christmas Novel. This is book number four in the series and my introduction to Judith Keim's writing. I wasn't disappointed. The characters are dimensional and engaging. The plot is well crafted and advances at a pleasing pace. The Florida location is interesting and warming. It was a delight to read a romance novel with mature female protagonists. Ann and Rhoda have life experiences that enrich the story. It's a clever book about friends and extended family. Buy copies for your book group pals and enjoy this seasonal read."*

MARGARITAS AT THE BEACH HOUSE HOTEL *– "What a wonderful series. I absolutely loved this book and can't wait for the next book to come out. There was even suspense in it. Thanks Judith for the great stories."*

"Overall, Margaritas at the Beach House Hotel is another wonderful addition to the series. Judith Keim takes the reader on a journey told through the voices of these amazing characters we have

all come to love through the years! I truly cannot stress enough how good this book is, and I hope you enjoy it as much as I have!"

THE HARTWELL WOMEN SERIES – Books 1 – 4

"This was an EXCELLENT series. When I discovered Judith Keim, I read all of her books back to back. I thoroughly enjoyed the women Keim has written about. They are believable and you want to just jump into their lives and be their friends! I can't wait for any upcoming books!"

"I fell into Judith Keim's Hartwell Women series and have read & enjoyed all of her books in every series. Each centers around a strong & interesting woman character and their family interaction. Good reads that leave you wanting more."

THE FAT FRIDAYS GROUP – Books 1 – 3

"Excellent story line for each character, and an insightful representation of situations which deal with some of the contemporary issues women are faced with today."

"I love this author's books. Her characters and their lives are realistic. The power of women's friendships is a common and beautiful theme that is threaded throughout this story."

THE SALTY KEY INN SERIES – Books 1 – 4

FINDING ME – *"I thoroughly enjoyed the first book in this series and cannot wait for the others! The characters are endearing with the same struggles we all encounter. The setting makes me feel like I am a guest at The Salty Key Inn...relaxed, happy & lighthearted! The men are yummy and the women strong. You can't get better than that! Happy Reading!"*

FINDING MY WAY- *"Loved the family dynamics as well as uncertain emotions of dating and falling in love. Appreciated the morals and strength of parenting throughout. Just couldn't put this book down."*

FINDING LOVE – *"I waited for this book because the first two was such good reads. This one didn't disappoint.... Judith Keim always puts substance into her books. This book was no different, I learned about PTSD, accepting oneself, there is always going to be problems but stick it out and make it work. Just the way life is. In some ways a lot like my life. Judith is right, it needs another book and I will definitely be reading it. Hope you choose to read this series, you will get so much out of it."*

FINDING FAMILY – *"Completing this series is like eating the last chip. Love Judith's writing, and her female characters are always smart, strong, vulnerable to life and love experiences."*

"This was a refreshing book. Bringing the heart and soul of the family to us."

CHANDLER HILL INN SERIES – Books 1 – 3

GOING HOME – *"I absolutely could not put this book down. Started at night and read late into the middle of the night. As a child of the '60s, the Vietnam war was front and center so this resonated with me. All the characters in the book were so well developed that the reader felt like they were friends of the family."*

"I was completely immersed in this book, with the beautiful descriptive writing, and the authors' way of bringing her characters to life. I felt like I was right inside her story."

COMING HOME – *"Coming Home is a winner. The characters are well-developed, nuanced and likable. Enjoyed the vineyard setting, learning about wine growing and seeing the challenges Cami faces in running and growing a business. I look forward to the next book in this series!"*

"Coming Home was such a wonderful story. The author has such a gift for getting the reader right to the heart of things."

HOME AT LAST – *"In this wonderful conclusion, to a heartfelt and emotional trilogy set in Oregon's stunning wine country, Judith Keim has tied up the Chandler Hill series with the perfect bow."*

"Overall, this is truly a wonderful addition to the Chandler Hill Inn series. Judith Keim definitely knows how to perfectly weave together a beautiful and heartfelt story."

"The storyline has some beautiful scenes along with family drama. Judith Keim has created characters with interactions that are believable and some of the subjects the story deals with are poignant."

SEASHELL COTTAGE BOOKS

A CHRISTMAS STAR – "Love, laughter, sadness, great food, and hope for the future, all in one book. It doesn't get any better than this stunning read."

"A Christmas Star is a heartwarming Christmas story featuring endearing characters. So many Christmas books are set in snowbound places...it was a nice change to read a Christmas story that takes place on a warm sandy beach!" Susan Peterson

CHANGE OF HEART – "CHANGE OF HEART is the summer read we've all been waiting for. Judith Keim is a master at creating fascinating characters that are simply irresistible. Her stories leave you with a big smile on your face and a heart bursting with love."

~Kellie Coates Gilbert, author of the popular Sun Valley Series

A SUMMER OF SURPRISES – "The story is filled with a roller coaster of emotions and self-discovery. Finding love again and rebuilding family relationships."

"Ms. Keim uses this book as an amazing platform to show that with hard emotional work, belief in yourself and love, the scars of abuse can be conquered. It in no way preaches, it's a lovely story with a happy ending."

"The character development was excellent. I felt I knew these people my whole life. The story development was very well thought out I was drawn [in] from the beginning."

A ROAD TRIP TO REMEMBER – "I LOVED this book! Love the character development, the fun, the challenges and the ending. My favorite books are about strong, competent women finding their own path to success and happiness and this is a winner. It's one of those books you just can't put down."

"The characters are so real that they jump off the page. Such a fun, HAPPY book at the perfect time. It will lift your spirits and even remind you of your own grandmother. Spirited and hopeful Aggie gets a second chance at love and she takes the steering wheel and drives straight for it."

DESERT SAGE INN BOOKS

THE DESERT FLOWERS – ROSE – *"The Desert Flowers - Rose, is the first book in the new series by Judith Keim. I always look forward to new books by Judith Keim, and this one is definitely a wonderful way to begin The Desert Sage Inn Series!"*

"In this first of a series, we see each woman come into her own and view new beginnings even as they must take this tearful journey as they slowly lose a dear friend. This is a very well written book with well-developed and likable main characters. It was interesting and enlightening as the first portion of this saga unfolded. I very much enjoyed this book and I do recommend it"

"Judith Keim is one of those authors that you can always depend on to give you a great story with fantastic characters. I'm excited to know that she is writing a new series and after reading book 1 in the series, I can't wait to read the rest of the books."!

THE DESERT FLOWERS – LILY –
"The second book in the Desert Flowers series is just as wonderful as the first. Judith Keim is a brilliant storyteller. Her characters are truly lovely and people that you want to be friends with as soon as you start reading. Judith Keim is not afraid to weave real life conflict and loss into her stories. I loved reading Lily's story and can't wait for Willow's!

"The Desert Flowers-Lily, is the second book in The Desert Sage Inn Series by author Judith Keim. When I read the first book in the series, The Desert Flowers-Rose, I knew this series would exceed all of my expectations and then some. Judith Keim is an amazing author, and this series is a testament to her writing skills and her ability to completely draw a reader into the world of her characters."

CHRISTMAS CASTLES

SOUL SISTERS AT CEDAR MOUNTAIN LODGE, BOOK 10

JUDITH KEIM

wildquail.pub@gmail.com
www.judithkeim.com

Wild Quail Publishing
PO Box 171332
Boise, ID 83717-1332

ISBN 978-1-954325-32-6

B

This book is dedicated to women everywhere who connect with others,
becoming sisters of the heart.

BOOKS BY JUDITH KEIM

THE HARTWELL WOMEN SERIES:

The Talking Tree – 1

Sweet Talk – 2

Straight Talk – 3

Baby Talk – 4

The Hartwell Women – Boxed Set

THE BEACH HOUSE HOTEL SERIES:

Breakfast at The Beach House Hotel – 1

Lunch at The Beach House Hotel – 2

Dinner at The Beach House Hotel – 3

Christmas at The Beach House Hotel – 4

Margaritas at The Beach House Hotel – 5

Dessert at The Beach House Hotel – 6 (2022)

THE FAT FRIDAYS GROUP:

Fat Fridays – 1

Sassy Saturdays – 2

Secret Sundays – 3

SALTY KEY INN SERIES:

Finding Me – 1

Finding My Way – 2

Finding Love – 3

Finding Family – 4

SEASHELL COTTAGE BOOKS:

A Christmas Star

Change of Heart

A Summer of Surprises

A Road Trip to Remember

The Beach Babes – (2022)

CHANDLER HILL INN BOOKS:

Going Home – 1

Coming Home – 2

Home at Last – 3

DESERT SAGE INN BOOKS:

The Desert Flowers – Rose – 1

The Desert Flowers – Lily – 2

The Desert Flowers – Willow – 3 (2022)

The Desert Flowers – Mistletoe & Holly – 4 (2022)

SOUL SISTERS AT CEDAR MOUNTAIN LODGE

Christmas Sisters – Anthology

Christmas Kisses

Christmas Castles

Christmas Stories – Soul Sisters Anthology

OTHER BOOKS

The ABC's of Living With a Dachshund

Once Upon a Friendship – Anthology

Winning BIG – a little love story for all ages

For more information: **www.judithkeim.com**

CHAPTER 1

Hailey Hensley walked on the beach in front of her house along the Gulf Coast of Florida. Thinking about her sisters brought a smile to her lips. How she loved them. Her Kirby soul sisters were married now and living and working with their spouses in Granite Ridge, Idaho, close to their mother, Maddie. Alissa and Stevie had babies—a boy and a girl for Alissa and a boy for Stevie. Becoming a mother was something she dearly wanted for herself. Though she and Nick had been trying, it hadn't happened. For Jo either.

On this late November morning, the air was cool, but the sun was warm. Zeke, her black-and-tan, smooth-haired dachshund, trotted ahead of her along the water's lacy edge. Behind him, his paw prints left their marks in the sand as he surveyed his surroundings. When the little sandpipers and other shorebirds skittering ahead of him didn't pay him proper attention, he barked and then raced to chase them away.

Above her, seagulls and terns circled and cried their messages to the world. The timeless soft slap of the waves hitting the beach and pulling away again filled Hailey with a sense of peace. Though it had been difficult to leave her family behind in Idaho, she loved living at the beach.

Nick wouldn't have asked her to move, but he was offered an opportunity to get an advanced degree in music education at the University of South Florida in Tampa and teach there. The other three members of his band, The Granite Rock Band, followed them to Florida. Several nights a month, they performed at various nightclubs in Ybor City and other clubs in the Tampa Bay area.

It was a good life. She loved Nick in a way she hadn't thought possible. He was a loving, generous, kind man who helped her realize that beneath her usual quiet demeanor lurked a woman capable of letting go and having fun. It was a new experience. Her early childhood in a series of foster homes before Maddie Kirby rescued her had been devoid of anything like joy. She'd even been afraid to speak aloud, which is why words and writing books were so important to her.

A thread of disappointment over the upcoming holidays wove through her, making her miss her family more than ever. For the first time, she and Nick would not gather with them in Granite Ridge for the Christmas holiday. Her mother and Nan would be on an extensive trip to Europe, Alissa and Jed planned to try to make peace with her in-laws out-of-town, and Stevie and Jo had other plans. Nick's sister, Stacy, and her daughter, Regan, were too busy at their candy shop in town to get away. She understood, but it was still a bit of a shock.

Her cell phone rang. She checked her caller ID. *Alissa.*

"Hey, there," said Hailey, her spirits lifting. "You're up early!"

"The baby woke up way too soon," Alissa said. "I'm still trying to get there. I thought I'd call while he's content, giving me time to sip my coffee while I talk to you. "What's new?"

"I'm working on my latest children's book. In this one,

Charlie and Zeke are making sandcastles and meeting a few seaside creatures. It's going to be a cute story."

"All your stories are lovely, Hailey. How's Nick? And Zeke?"

"Nick is at school and Zeke is trying to make the shoreline his private kingdom by running and chasing the birds away."

Alissa chuckled. "He's adorable. It was so cute of Nick to surprise you with a real Zeke a couple of years ago. It'll be great to see you all. I can't wait for our girls' weekend in April. I'm dragging a bit."

"I'll set aside all those days, and we can do whatever you want," Hailey said happily.

"Even if it means sitting and napping?" teased Alissa.

"Yes, that too."

"Oops! Gotta go," said Alissa. "It's going to be a very different Christmas for all of us, but I'll be thinking of you."

"Me, too. Love you," said Hailey, fighting an unexpected sting of tears.

"Love you too," Alissa managed to say before clicking off as Hailey heard a baby cry. Hailey slid her palm across her abdomen, wondering if she was ever going to nurture a baby there.

She looked up as Janna Underwood walked down the beach toward her.

Hailey lifted a hand and waved. Janna worked at the President Barack Obama Main Library in St. Petersburg, and they'd become good friends. Though she was busy with her book projects, Hailey volunteered to work in the children's section of the library every week and to participate in storytimes for toddlers, a favorite age group of hers.

"How are you? How did your date go last night?" Hailey said.

Janna made a face. "He didn't say he wanted to meet up again. But I was introduced to another person in the group, a man named Mike Garrett, who teaches at the same school as

Nick. He's a psychologist who has his own practice but teaches too. Still, I don't expect anything to come of it."

"I'm sorry," Hailey said. Janna's love life was a series of mishaps and unsuitable men. At almost six feet tall with long red hair that she most often wore in a ponytail, Janna had a stunning face and a body a model would envy.

"Thanks." Janna sighed.

Hailey smiled. Friends like Janna couldn't replace her sisters, but they meant a lot to her. "The right man will come along for you, Janna. I'm sure of it."

"If only. Well, I've got to move, or I'll be late for work. See you later."

Janna went on her way, and Hailey continued her walk. Moving briskly on the hard-packed sand at the edge of the water was great exercise not only for her body but for her brain. Some of her best story ideas came during times like this.

She was deep in thought when Zeke's bark caught her attention. She looked up at the sight of a little girl she guessed to be four standing at the edge of the water throwing a handful of shells into the oncoming waves.

A man walked over, stood next to the girl, and spoke softly to her.

Hailey had no idea what the man said to her, but the girl threw her arms around his legs and hugged him.

Zeke, curious as always, ran over to them.

The man lifted the girl into his arms and turned to Hailey. "Is your dog friendly?"

Hailey grinned at them. "He's safe from everything but kisses. But, if you'd like, I'll put his leash on him and lead him away."

"No, Daddy! I want to pet him." The girl wiggled out of his arms and faced her. "Can I touch him?"

Hailey snapped Zeke's leash on and nodded. "He loves tummy rubs."

The little girl reached out a hand, and Zeke licked it. Then he rolled over on his back and wagged his tail energetically, waiting for the attention he thought was due him.

Hailey laughed softly at his typical dachshund antics and observed the little girl squat beside Zeke and gently rub his stomach.

"That's right. He likes that." Hailey noticed the tender smile on the man's face and said, "I should introduce myself. I'm Hailey Hensley."

"I'm Michael Garrett, and this is my daughter, Zoey."

"Oh my gosh! My friend Janna Underwood and I were just talking about you. You teach at the University of South Florida in Tampa like my husband, Nick. He teaches music."

"Interesting. I work with the psychology program there," he said, helping Zoey to her feet. "Perhaps we'll bump into one another." Tall, with regular, pleasant features, bright blue eyes, and a headful of light-brown curls, he was an attractive man. More than that, she sensed kindness about him. *No wonder Janna was attracted to him*, Hailey thought.

"I'll tell Nick to look you up." Hailey hesitated, and then, thinking of Janna, she said, "By the way, I volunteer at the Barack Obama Main Library and will be doing a story hour there this afternoon at three. Any chance you could bring Zoey? I'd love to have her join us."

"Let me see about that. I'm a single dad, but Zoey's babysitter might be able to bring her. I'll ask. Thank you." He turned to Zoey. "C'mon, sweetie, we have to go. Time for me to leave for work."

"Okay, but I want a dog like Zeke. He's the best," said Zoey. With her dark curly hair and sparkling hazel eyes, she was adorable.

"We'll see about that. Say goodbye to Mrs. Hensley. You might see her later at the library."

"Really? Will Zeke be there, too?" said Zoey.

"He's in the storybook I'll be reading, but he won't be at the library," I said.

Mike's eyebrows raised. "Are you talking about the Charlie and Zeke books?"

"Yes," she answered cautiously.

"I've read all of them myself and read them to Zoey. They're an excellent choice for children, full of reaffirming ideas."

"I'm glad to hear that," Hailey said, not willing to let on that she was the author. She might have come out of her shell a lot since she'd been Zoey's age, but she was still uneasy about revealing too much too quickly about herself. That's why she used the pen name, Lee Merriweather.

"Thanks for sharing your dog with Zoey," said Mike. "Nice meeting you."

"For me, too," said Hailey and watched them head away from the beach to one of the nearby parking areas.

On the way back to her house, Hailey thought of the coincidence of meeting Mike after hearing about him from Janna. She smiled to herself. Maybe, by inviting Zoey to storytime, nice things would happen to her friend.

That afternoon, Hailey was thrilled to see Zoey show up with an older woman who was, no doubt, her babysitter. She went over to her. "I'm glad to see Zoey here. I invited her to come this morning."

The woman smiled at her. "Yes, Zoey's father told me about it. That's why we're here. I'm Nellie Davis."

"I'm Hailey Hensley, a volunteer here. The storytime lasts about 45 minutes. That's as long as most kids in the group can handle, with a few rests in between. You can either join us or take a break elsewhere."

"Thanks. I have some errands to run. Zoey's father will pick up Zoey," said Nellie.

"Okay," said Hailey, but her mind raced. Janna often left early on Tuesdays. She'd have to keep her here at the library on some pretext.

The children's area quickly filled, and Hailey's attention was diverted when a pregnant woman arrived with a little boy about Zoey's age. "Can I leave him for storytime? I have some errands to run and he'll be much happier here."

"Sure," said Hailey. "I'll keep him with me until you return." The poor woman looked frazzled.

Hailey took hold of his hand. "What's your name?"

"He's Brady," the woman said. "He doesn't speak too often; he's on the shy side."

"Okay, Brady, come with me, and you can sit in the circle with the other kids."

He looked up at Hailey with big, round brown eyes and studied her for a moment before nodding.

Hailey squeezed his hand, understanding his shyness.

Brady followed her to the circle of chairs where Shawna Wheeler, the assistant librarian, was helping the other children get settled. Brady sat close to Hailey.

"You're doing fine right here," Hailey said quietly, remembering when one of her foster parents had dropped her off at a daycare center without even saying good bye.

Hailey faced the children. "Shall we begin our story?" she asked and then laughed at the chorus of "yeses" that followed.

"What are Charlie and Zeke up to now?" asked one of the children, giving her a worried look as she opened one of her earlier books.

"I bet he's going to get into more trouble," Zoey said grinning.

Hailey clapped her hand for silence. "Let's see. Shall we?" She'd written several books about Charlie and his dachshund, Zeke, who often found themselves in all kinds of troubles as they learned one life lesson after another. Each book had a happy ending, of course, because she understood how important that was.

Hailey loved to see children caught up in a story and worked hard to act out the story. As she turned the last page, she read:

"Charlie's mother hugged him. "I'm so glad you came home. I missed you."

"I promise not to run away again," said Charlie. He hadn't been gone long. After going only one block with his dachshund, Zeke, he wished he hadn't done it. As his mother had told him, "Home is where the heart is," and he knew his home was with her and the rest of his family."

Whenever Hailey got to this part of the story, her eyes stung with tears remembering how she'd felt the first time she'd known she was a true member of a family—the family Maddie Kirby had brought together. It was another reason she wanted children of her own.

Hailey gave the kids a chance to get up and move around by playing a short game of standing and sitting to different words. Then she began another story. This time, the book was about a pig who wanted to fly.

Toward the end of the story, she saw Janna headed for the exit and called out to her. "Please stay. There's something we need to talk about."

"Can it wait?" asked Janna.

"Absolutely not," Hailey said, eyeing Zoey.

Janna shrugged and headed back to her office.

Later, when Hailey observed Mike and Janna staring at each other with growing smiles, Hailey couldn't help the satisfied feeling that filled her. Their delight at seeing each other was so apparent, she clasped her hands and sighed. Her soul sisters shared looks like that with the men they'd married.

As she had promised, Hailey waited with Brady for his mother to return. Hailey tried talking to him about the stories they'd read, but though he listened, he didn't respond to the questions she posed. Hailey understood and continued talking, knowing her words were making an impact, anyway.

His mother appeared twenty minutes or so later, out of breath. "I'm so sorry. Traffic was worse than normal. I'm not sure why. It's a little early for tourist season."

"It's not a problem. I've enjoyed talking with Brady," Hailey said. She studied Brady's mother. Of average height, she was pretty in a classic way with shoulder-length, dark hair and eyes a pretty shade of green.

"Thanks again. I won't keep you any longer," Brady's mother said.

Hailey patted Brady's shoulder. "He's a very nice boy. He can come to storytime anytime he and you want. By the way, I'm Hailey Hensley."

"Linnie," Brady's mother said, smiling shyly. "Thanks. I'll bring him next week. We love coming to the library."

"Okay, then. Next week, Brady," said Hailey giving him a quick hug.

Brady's arm slowly came around Hailey's body.

"Wow!" said Linnie, her eyes round. "You're really great with kids. Brady usually doesn't warm up to someone so quickly."

"I love children," Hailey said.

"How many do you have?" Linnie asked.

Hailey felt heat creeping into her cheeks. "None yet. But we're trying."

Linnie sighed and patted her protruding stomach. "This one was a surprise. No one was happy about it. Especially Brady's dad. Just another few weeks to go."

"Good luck with everything," Hailey said, feeling a stab of sadness for the baby not yet born.

"Thanks again. See you next week," said Linnie taking hold of Brady's hand and leading him away, juggling her shopping bags awkwardly.

Happy she'd see Brady again Hailey left the library anxious to get home to Nick.

She'd just pulled her car into the garage when her cell rang. She clicked on the call.

"Thanks," said Janna, "I'm going out with Mike this weekend."

Hailey laughed. "I knew it."

"I'll meet you on the beach tomorrow and tell you all about it. Deal?"

"Deal," said Hailey, getting out of the car and smiling as Nick and Zeke hurried toward her.

CHAPTER 2

The next morning, Hailey kissed Nick goodbye. "Have a nice day. And remember to look up Mike Garrett. He and Janna are going out on a date this weekend. He seems like a really nice guy. If things work out between them, I'd like to invite the two of them to dinner."

"Little Miss Matchmaker, are we?" teased Nick wrapping his arms around her and holding her close.

She rested her head against his chest, loving the manly smell of him, the secure feeling he gave her. Being in his arms always made her feel special.

"I'll treat you to one of Maddie's favorite dishes for dinner," she said. "I'm feeling domestic after last night." She grinned. "Practice makes perfect for so many things."

He grinned and cupped her cheeks in his hands. "I'm glad we talked about not worrying about your getting pregnant and just enjoying ourselves. It takes a lot of pressure off." He lowered his lips to hers. "You're going to be the best mom ever."

At Zeke's yipping, they pulled apart.

"Such a jealous guy," said Nick, patting Zeke's head. "He has every right to be."

Hailey laughed at Zeke's look of satisfaction. "See you later, Nick."

After he left, Hailey put the dishes in the dishwasher, checked the clock, called to Zeke, and headed out the door to meet Janna.

On the porch, Hailey picked up the plastic bucket and utensils she used for making sandcastles. She never got tired of molding the sand into different shapes. It opened up her mind to possible story ideas— in both words and pictures.

Even now, as she walked along the beach, her painter's eye saw things others might miss—the way the sun capped the waves with sparkling crowns, the curvature of seagulls' wings against the cobalt blue of the sky, the intricate patterns of the footprints different shorebirds and creatures left behind in the sand.

A sigh of happiness escaped her. She might miss her family, but she came alive with the sights and sounds around her, and she loved the comparative warmth.

She saw Janna in the distance and waved, eager to talk to her friend. The idea that Janna wanted to speak to her about Mike was intriguing. She usually held back information on upcoming dates.

When they met up, Hailey gave Janna a quick hug. "Okay, tell me everything about your conversation with Mike."

Janna beamed at her. "Well, it didn't end at the library. He offered to take me to coffee, and he, Zoey, and I went to Cuppa down the street. We talked for a long time. Zoey was so well behaved. She had a treat and then looked at pictures in one of the books she checked out from the library while Mike talked about his childhood growing up. He'd already told me his wife died in childbirth with Zoey. He said when he finally decided to date, some of the younger women he met didn't like the idea of dealing with a toddler."

"Wow! It sounds like he was very open with you," Hailey said.

Janna nodded and smiled. "I told him I was tired of dating guys who didn't like it when I spoke up about social issues, that I wanted to be more than a pretty date on someone's arm, someone who was expected to turn into a sex-starved play-mate at the end of it."

"What did Mike say to that?" Hailey asked.

"He laughed. He's so darn cute," said Janna. "And easy to talk to."

Hailey touched Janna's arm. "I'm happy for you. But I remember how excited you've been about other men. I hope you're not rushing things or pushing too hard."

"This time is different. There's a connection between us I can't describe."

"I asked Nick to look up Mike on campus. If everything works out the way you want, it might be fun to double-date."

"Yes. Oh, Hailey, this is so exciting!"

"I need to ask you about Brady and his mother, Linnie. What do you know about them?"

"The little boy who doesn't talk?" Janna said. "Linnie MacGrath has been coming to the library with Brady for a few months. I'm not sure what's going on with her. I've never seen her with anyone else. Funny, I've always wondered if she had a secretive life; she looks so sad and beautiful, like a tragic character in a book. But then you know how imagina-tive I can be about people."

Hailey laughed. "You're almost as bad as I am weaving stories about people I meet."

"I don't know much about her, but Linnie seems like a good mom. Brady doesn't often speak, but he clearly loves her," said Janna.

"Yes, he was happy to see his mother. And before he left, he hugged me," Hailey said.

"Really? Hailey, you have such a sweet way with kids. They adore you," Janna pointed to the bucket and shovels Hailey was carrying. "I see you have your sandcastle tools with you. I've seen some of your sandcastles. They're so interesting with all the turrets and towers you create."

"Thanks. I thought it might help me tell Charlie's story at the seashore. I've done some paintings for the books, but I want to get the right words to match them."

"No matter what you do, I know it'll be a fascinating book for children. They love discovering the little details on each page. Sort of like a Richard Scarry book, yet so uniquely you."

"Thanks for your confidence." Those details here and there made her paintings easy to discuss with children.

"I'd better go. Have fun with your castles," said Janna. "See you later."

Hailey called to Zeke and clipped his leash on him so he wouldn't follow Janna. She liked to keep him close while working on her sandcastles. She got so caught up in the project she lost track of time and even Zeke sometimes. Nick teased her about it.

Now, working on her sandcastle, Hailey thought about Linnie and her little boy. She hadn't told Janna, but it had bothered her that Brady's father didn't seem to want the baby.

Her thoughts flew to Nick. He was such a strong father figure for his niece, Regan, that she knew how fantastic he'd be with children of his own. It had been something important to her during their whirlwind romance. With many compatible thoughts about life and how they wanted to live, along with undeniable chemistry, it was no wonder they fell quickly and so deeply in love.

As if her thoughts had brought him to life, she looked up and saw Nick strolling down the beach toward her, the breeze rumpling his hair. Zeke, eager to get to him, barked and pulled on his leash wrapped around her ankle, flipping her on her backside. Laughing, she undid the leash and let Zeke take off in a flurry of paws against the sand.

"When I didn't see you in your studio, I figured I'd find

you here," said Nick, pulling her up to her feet and wrapping his arms around her.

They kissed, and then Hailey and Nick simply smiled at one another.

Zeke barked for attention.

"Hold on, buddy," said Nick. "I'm just saying hello to your mom."

Zeke whimpered and lay down, giving them a doleful look.

"The world is not ending, Zeke," Hailey chided. She turned to Nick. "You're home early."

"My professor canceled class, and my private-tutoring student asked to delay the lesson until tomorrow. So, I'm here to play with you." Nick's dark eyes sparkled with mischief. "I like your sandcastles. Want help with this one?"

"They're more than sandcastles, you know. I fill them with hopes and dreams for the people I place inside them." Hailey looked at the half-built castle at her feet and laughed. "No, I have to get home and make some notes on what I've decided I need to add to my book in both pictures and descriptions."

She stopped and gazed at the water before turning to him with a shy smile.

He pulled her to him. "I love you, Hailey. You're such a special person."

She hugged him back, grateful he appreciated her whimsy. Her sisters used to say she reminded them of a tiny fairy with her strawberry-blond hair, big blue eyes, and the way she seemed to dance on her feet with quick, lithe movements. She sometimes thought of herself that way as she brushed strokes of color on blank paper. Her watercolors in her children's books echoed that feeling, lending them a magical quality.

"I'll walk you back, and maybe we can go out to lunch or something. By the way, I met Mike Garrett this morning. He seems like a nice guy."

"Janna's in love. I hope Mike won't break her heart," Hailey said. "I've never seen her this way."

"They'll work it out for themselves," Nick said, taking hold of her hand. "Hungry? Where should we go?"

"How about Gracie's at the Salty Key Inn?" Hailey loved the story of the three sisters who owned the hotel and the group of people who ran the restaurant.

"Sounds great," said Nick, smiling at her.

As they walked on, she felt at home on the sand with Nick at her side. It had been a shock when he'd asked her to move to Florida, but she'd grown to love it. Besides, it pleased her that he was happy in school and with his work.

"Look," said Nick, pointing out over the water.

A trio of pelicans flew low to the water, searching for food.

Pelicans had quickly become some of her favorite shorebirds. They looked like performers in a U.S. Navy Blue Angels show as they skimmed the water's surface, swooping to dive into it to gather food in their unique beaks.

"I need to add so many more images to my book," Hailey said, laughing as another pelican seemed to stand on his head before plunging into the water.

Nick put his arm around her. "I'm glad you like it here, Hailey. I know it's been an adjustment for you to be away from your family."

Hailey nodded thoughtfully. "It's true, but we're all spreading our wings, so to speak, which is, as Maddie says, the way it should be."

"She's such an inspiring woman," he said.

"She truly is," Hailey replied. "I met an interesting little boy and his mother at the library yesterday, and I've been doing a lot of thinking about them. The little boy is adorable but doesn't speak. He reminded me of myself at that age. And there's something sad about the mother. I want to know more about them."

"This isn't going to turn into another project of yours, is it?"

Hailey laughed. "Not really. Just curious."

They returned to their house. Before they left for Gracie's, Hailey went into her studio and made some notes about images and narratives to add to the book. Her agent sometimes was impatient with her for taking so long to create each book, but Hailey wanted to make sure every one of them was as perfect as she could make it.

They left Zeke whining at the kitchen door to join them, got into Nick's truck, and drove up Gulf Boulevard to the Salty Key Inn. The inn's gourmet restaurant, Gavin's, was well known in the area for outstanding dinners and excellent catering for special events. Gracie's was open for breakfast and lunch and was just as popular for its homestyle menu.

They pulled into the almost-full parking lot and found a space for the truck just before two more cars entered the lot.

"Crowded as usual," Nick said, climbing out of the truck.

Hailey joined him, and they walked to the front door, where a colorful, carved-wood statue of a sea captain greeted them.

When they stepped inside, an older woman smiled at them. "Table for two?"

Hailey nodded. "Pretty crowded today. Can we have a table on the patio?"

"Sure, honey. A couple just left there," said the waitress whose nametag indicated she was Dolly. She led them to a table outside, where the buzz of conversation filled the air.

Hailey took a seat opposite Nick and let out a sigh of happiness. Though it wasn't hot, the combination of fresh air and sunshine was perfect.

"We just got some fresh grouper in, and everyone is raving about our special grouper sandwiches," said Dolly. "Fair warning. It's going fast."

"Save one for me, please," said Nick, as Dolly filled their glasses with water.

"Will do," said Dolly. "Now, what else can I get you?"

Nick and Hailey ordered iced tea, then Hailey ordered the chicken salad plate. It was her favorite. Pineapple chunks, slivered almonds, and distinctive island seasonings made Gracie's chicken salad special. That, served with a homemade roll and fresh fruit, was a best seller.

While they waited to be served, Nick told Hailey about an idea he had for a class he was teaching in the spring.

She listened carefully, liking the way Nick's face lit up at the prospect of introducing music to new students. She loved that about him. He'd once been a superstar on the rock concert circuit adored by a legion of females. He gave up the lifestyle of a touring bandmember when he came home to Granite Ridge to help his sister, Stacy, run the family candy store. Now, Nick was content teaching others. He'd often told her he'd never go back on the road, but the gigs he and his fellow band members played in the area were special events for them all.

As they ate their meal, Hailey noticed a few people around them staring at Nick. He was a handsome man well known for his music. She and Nick had learned to ignore the attention that he received. As Nick had once told her, she was far more famous than he'd ever been. People just didn't know she was also Lee Merriweather, a famous children's book author.

"When we get home, will you help me wrap Christmas gifts for the family?" Hailey asked. "I'm down to the last few packages."

"Let me guess, one more surprise for each sister?"

Hailey gave him a sheepish look. "It's just that I won't see them this year."

"No problem. I gave Stacy our order for Christmas Kisses to be delivered to each of their households."

"Thanks." Hailey smiled, remembering how his sister Stacy had encouraged Hailey to reach out to Nick. She'd admired him for years but didn't think he'd ever be interested in her. When they finally got together, they fell for each other fast.

CHAPTER 3

S unday morning, as Hailey was relaxing by the pool with a cup of coffee, her cell chimed. *Janna.*

Hailey snatched up her phone. "How did it go?"

"My date with Mike was delightful," sighed Janna. "He and I really enjoyed ourselves. We went to the movies and out for a drink afterward."

"And then?" Hailey asked.

"And then he came inside," said Janna. She let out a little squeal. "He wants to take me out on Wednesday."

"Great," said Hailey. "I'm glad things are going so well. Would you consider coming to dinner here next Saturday? Nick liked Mike, and it might be nice for them. Besides, you know I'm dying to see you two together."

Janna laughed. "Dinner sounds nice. It would be interesting to see how Mike is in a small group. And I want your input."

"Okay, then. Let's do it. Nick isn't playing in the band next weekend, and we wanted to plan something special."

Nick came out to the lanai as Hailey ended the call. She filled him in on the plans, and he said, "Okay. Fine with me."

"We need to meet new couples. We tend to stay at home a

lot except when you're working with the band." Hailey grinned. "It does my heart good to hear Janna so excited. The dating apps aren't always the best way to meet compatible people. Sometimes it takes Zeke meeting a little girl to make things happen."

Nick chuckled. "So now Zeke is the matchmaker."

"Looks that way," said Hailey, rubbing Zeke's ears.

When Hailey walked into the library for story hour the following week, she was surprised to see Brady and Linnie already there.

Linnie walked over to her. "After story hour, can we talk?"

"Sure," said Hailey. "We can go to Cuppa's for coffee afterward. Does that sound okay?"

"Yes, that will be perfect," said Linnie.

Hailey studied her and realized Linnie was acting nervous. Her curiosity ratcheted up.

Brady looked up at her.

"Are you ready for another story?" she asked him.

"Yes," he answered softly and took the hand she offered him.

He sat in a chair next to her while other children found seats in chairs or sat on the floor.

As she gazed at the circle of eager faces around her, Hailey's heart filled with affection. She loved children and the joy they got from simple things, like having a story read to them. It's why she took such care with each of her books.

After the final story had been read and the children had helped resettle the chairs in their proper places, Hailey said goodbye to one of the librarians and left the building with Linnie and Brady.

Following a short walk, they entered Cuppa's coffee shop. Hailey inhaled the aroma of coffee. She loved coming here. She often treated herself to a mocha drink and sometimes one of their delicious muffins. Blueberry/almond was her favorite.

Hailey ordered and turned to Linnie. "Go ahead and get whatever you want for you and Brady, my treat."

"Oh, but ..." Linnie said.

"It's a pleasant surprise for me to have more time with you and Brady," Hailey said. "I'm happy to pay."

"Thank you," Linnie said and placed their order.

After getting settled at a table near the window, Linnie pulled out a coloring book and crayons from her large purse and placed them in front of Brady. "You color while Hailey and I talk." She handed him the cookie he'd wanted.

Watching closely, Hailey took a sip of her coffee. Brady seemed like such an easy kid.

"Thank you for agreeing to meet with me. It means a lot. One of the librarians told me you wrote the Charlie and Zeke stories. Since then, I've done a little research on you and learned about your time in foster care. I'm a product of foster care too."

Hailey studied her. "Interesting. I'm sure we have a lot of similar stories to tell one another. I was one of the lucky kids because I was adopted when I was eight. Back then, I was like Brady and didn't talk much. That's why I'm fascinated with him. In foster care, I learned not to talk. Every time I did, I got into trouble. But his isn't the same situation at all," Hailey said. "How long were you in the system?"

"From age seven until I left my placement when I was seventeen. It was a horrible experience," said Linnie. Sadness crept across her face. "I had a few okay homes, but they never lasted."

Observing Linnie's pain, Hailey reached over and clasped her hand. "I'm so sorry. A lovely woman took me into her home and adopted me with three other girls. I'll always be thankful for her."

"Yeah, I read about that in your bio. I entered foster care when my grandmother died. Both of my parents were out of the picture. Meth use, among other things."

Hailey studied Linnie. She was an attractive woman with shiny dark hair, green eyes, healthy skin, and a fashion flare that suited her. Her heart went out to her.

"I just wanted to thank you for being so kind to Brady. We've lived here only a few months, and we haven't had time to make any real friends."

Hailey smiled. "And now you have."

A pretty flush colored Linnie's cheeks. "Thank you."

"Why did you come to the Gulf Coast of Florida?"

"To see someone," Linnie said. "I'm still not sure it was the right move. Time will tell."

Hailey was dying to ask more about it but decided Linnie would tell her when she was ready. For the moment, it felt good to sit and simply chat. Writing and illustrating books was a lonely career. She loved it, but having grown up in a household of women, she missed the chatter of female friends.

Hailey turned to Brady, who was coloring a picture of a dog. "Are you making him brown and black like Zeke?"

He smiled at her and nodded. "Yes. Like Zeke. But this dog isn't long and skinny like Zeke."

Surprised at his speech, Hailey glanced at Linnie.

She looked as surprised as Hailey felt. A huge smile crossed her face. "That's good, Brady. I like how you can talk to Ms. Hailey." Linnie checked her watch and gave Hailey an apologetic look. "We'd better go. I work at home doing online data entry for a company."

"Thank you for inviting me today. Maybe we can do it again," said Hailey, pleased with her interaction with Brady.

"That would be lovely," said Linnie. "Again, thank you so much for your kindness."

Hailey said goodbye to them but remained seated at the table to finish her coffee and muffin. Linnie had opened up a little, but Hailey knew there was much more to her story.

As the days flew by, Hailey focused on the seaside book she was working on for Charlie and Zeke. In this story, Zeke drags a bottle holding a message from the water, and Charlie finds a new friend.

By the time the weekend arrived, Hailey was happy to set aside studio work and get ready for the Saturday evening dinner with Janna and Mike. After moving to Florida, she and Janna, with their shared interest in books and their love of the beach, had quickly become friends. Janna was a foodie and enjoyed sharing new recipes with her, so Hailey wanted to cook a special meal. After much thought, she decided on grilled snapper, grilled veggies, and a spinach and strawberry salad. For dessert, every man she knew loved something chocolate, so she prepared *chocolate pots de crème*.

That morning, she set the dining room table. Though the table could hold as many as twelve with all the leaves inserted, she kept it small so the four of them would feel cozy sitting together. She put fresh candles in the glass candlesticks her mother had given her one Christmas and placed the empty glass hibiscus-blossom holder between them. At the last minute, she'd pick a fresh blossom and insert it inside. She folded crisp linen napkins and set one between the silverware on each pink and green floral placemat. As if he knew guests were coming, Zeke watched her every move and followed her from room to room as she freshened them.

Hailey was proud of the house they'd bought and grateful too. Maybe that's why she was so fascinated with sandcastles and loved to build elaborate ones. Though they had a landscaping team come in every week, Nick liked to fuss around the yard by himself from time to time. Living in a subtropical climate meant a constant race to keep everything trimmed and looking well-tended.

Later, just before Janna and Mike were due to arrive, Hailey walked outside and chose a lovely pink hibiscus bloom to put in the holder on the dining room table.

Standing back, observing the effect, Hailey was satisfied. Now she was ready.

The sound of the doorbell carried through the house. Zeke barked and ran to the front door.

Hailey and Nick followed.

Nick opened the door and stood back.

Hailey hugged Janna and turned to Mike. "I'm so happy you agreed to come tonight. You know Nick."

"Yes. Nice to see you again." Mike and Nick shook hands.

Janna handed her two bottles of wine. "I didn't know what you were serving, so we brought both red and white."

"How thoughtful! It's going to be so nice to be able to sit and relax with you and a glass of wine. Come on in."

Janna dutifully patted Zeke on the head before following Hailey inside.

"Zoey sure loved this little guy," said Mike rubbing Zeke's ears.

"She was very gentle with him," Hailey said, remembering how eagerly Zoey had rubbed Zeke's tummy.

"I suppose one day we'll get a dog, but not for a while," Mike said.

"I'd get a dachshund like Zeke any day if I didn't have to work full time," said Janna.

Zeke looked up at her and barked as if telling her she was foolish to wait.

Hailey joined the laughter as she led Janna and Mike through the kitchen and out to the lanai beyond it.

"What would everyone like to drink?" Nick said. "The bar is open. Janna? Mike? Hailey?"

Janna opted for a glass of white wine while Mike chose a gin and tonic.

Holding her glass of wine, Hailey settled on the couch with Janna. "How was your week?" she asked Janna.

"It was busy, which I always like," Janna said. "Brady and Linnie came in a couple of times. I think as the time approaches for her to have her baby, she finds it a quiet, peaceful place for both of them."

Hailey told Janna about having coffee with Linnie and Brady. "Linnie is such an interesting person. She's a product of foster care, like me."

"She seems lovely," Janna said, "and Brady is beginning to open up by being there."

The men came and sat down after viewing the grill setup Nick had.

"Been watching the Dolphins?" Mike asked Nick.

"You bet. That Mac MacGrath is something else. Talk about a comeback—from drugs to rehab and back to stardom. He's so quick to size up the situation on the field. No wonder he's heading for player of the year."

"He's a favorite of mine, too," said Mike. "I'm always interested in seeing how someone handles the aftermath of instant stardom. He's one helluva football player."

Hailey got to her feet. "While you men talk about football, I'm going to get dinner started."

"I'll come with you," said Janna.

In the kitchen, Janna turned to Hailey. "What do you think? Isn't Mike terrific?"

Hailey grinned and nodded. The attraction between the two of them was obvious.

"His mother is taking Zoey for a sleepover tonight, a

special treat for her. If Mike asks to spend the night, I'm going to say yes."

"Things are happening that fast?" said Hailey.

Janna face brightened. "Up to now, we've mostly just kissed and cuddled and talked. We've shared everything from our childhoods to the present day. Because of his profession, he's more open than most men would be." Janna hesitated, then said, "Do you believe in soulmates?"

Hailey glanced outside to where Nick was sitting with Mike. "I certainly do."

"Fantastic," said Janna. "Me too."

After one of the most pleasant evenings Hailey had enjoyed recently, she snuggled up against Nick in bed. "It makes me happy to see how comfortable Mike and Janna are with one another."

"They're great together," Nick said, gently rubbing Hailey's back. "Like you and me."

Hailey chuckled. "No one else can match us."

"True," Nick murmured, lowering his lips to hers.

As always, when Hailey was in his arms kissing him, her heart filled with such love she felt close to crying. She knew it had something to do about feeling unloved in her formative years and decided simply to accept it.

Nick, sensitive to her feelings, hugged her closer and whispered, "I love you."

CHAPTER 4

Hailey's work week started with a phone call from Rachel Robbins, her new editor. "How is the book coming along? Any chance we could have it by New Year's Day?"

"No, but I promise that no matter what I'll have it ready by Valentine's Day," Hailey said, rolling her eyes.

"That's a promise I expect you to keep," said Rachel. "Gotta go but thought we might have a chance to move the book into an earlier slot."

Hailey got off the call feeling disgruntled. Her original agreement called for the book to be sent to her editor by April 15th. Sighing, she went back to her painting.

By the time her weekly storytime session came, Hailey was as excited as one of the kids. She headed to the library with a new book she'd ordered online. It was a follow-up to the pig who wanted to fly. In this book, the pig wanted to dance.

As the kids were getting settled, Linnie and Brady arrived. He waved at her and came right over to her side.

"Hi, there, Brady. Have a seat right by me."

He folded his legs and sat on the floor by her chair. Hailey waved goodbye to Linnie and turned to the kids. "Ready for another story?"

Brady's "yes!" was as loud as the others.

Smiling with satisfaction, Hailey began.

Later, Hailey approached Linnie. "Want to go for coffee again? My treat?"

Linnie beamed a response. "I need something to sip on and could use some company."

They left the building and headed to Cuppa's comfortable with one another.

Inside the restaurant, Linnie and Brady found a free table while Hailey placed their orders.

Observing them from a distance, Hailey filled with curiosity once more. Brady was a handsome little boy who was talking more freely now. His mother loved him and treated him with respect. Hailey couldn't help wondering what they were doing in this area. Linnie had mentioned meeting someone. But who?

After their drinks and treats were served and Brady was content with a handheld game, Hailey turned to Linnie. "How are things going?"

Linnie sighed and set down her cup of tea. "I'm here on this coast of Florida trying to keep out of sight, away from the public's eyes in case I can't work things out with Brady's father, Mac. He and I were married five years ago. But we'd known each other long before that. He's a foster care kid, too. Being married was a happy time for us. When Brady arrived, we were ecstatic. And then stardom and drugs became part of the scene, and I divorced him. Nine months ago, we reunited for a weekend, and then this happened." Linnie indicated her belly with a gentle rub. "Mac was furious with me for getting pregnant. He thinks I allowed it to happen because I'm after his money."

"Whoa," said Hailey. "What are you talking about? Who is Mac?"

"Maybe you've heard of him. He's 'Mac' MacGrath, who plays for the Miami Dolphins."

"Really?" said Hailey. "My husband, Nick, was talking about him recently. He's a huge fan of his. Nick told the story about his being suspended and making a comeback. Now Mac's his favorite superstar." She'd seen pictures of him. He was a ruggedly handsome man with an impish smile that served him well.

Linnie nodded grimly. "I didn't want to divorce Mac; I love him. I always have and always will. But I couldn't stay and risk Brady's getting hurt because of his father's actions when he was drinking and drugging. That's why I left him. After we left, Mac went into rehab."

"And now?" Hailey said.

"Now, I'm talking to him to see if there's any chance of our getting back together."

"But he has a girlfriend, some supermodel," Hailey said. She knew this because they'd talked about it at dinner last weekend. Mike was as big a fan of Mac as Nick.

"I don't think it's the real thing," said Linnie. "She's not his type, no matter what she's telling the press. Talk about someone going after his money! Whether we get back together or not, Mac needs to see Brady, and we need to continue discussing the situation."

"That's some story," said Hailey, her mind spinning.

"I thought it would be helpful if you knew what was going on, so if the opportunity came to talk to Brady about his father, you would know the truth."

"Does Brady get along with his father?" Hailey asked.

"Even though he hasn't seen him for several months, he still talks about him occasionally, but almost in a disconnected way. After we left him in Miami, Brady stopped talking about him and other things too. We've both had a lot of trauma lately. Brady talks from time to time, but not like he used to, and usually not with strangers. He really likes you, Hailey."

"And I like him," said Hailey. "If you need me to watch Brady while you visit his father sometime, I'd be happy to help out."

Linnie's eyes widened and then filled with tears. "You'd do that for us?"

"Sure. If it'll help Brady, I'm happy to do it."

Linnie gave her a shaky smile. "Has anyone ever told you you're an angel?"

Hailey laughed. "Not recently." She studied Brady. "What are you going to do when you have the baby?"

"I haven't figured that out yet. We've been in this area for only a few months. Not long enough to make any real friends. You understand."

"Yes, I do," Hailey said honestly. It usually took her a while to make friends, but when she did, it was forever. "How are you getting by?"

"Right now, I'm doing some data entry and online marketing work at home for a clothing catalog, but it doesn't go far. We have some money from Mac. If things don't work out with him, I might take Brady back to Indiana where a job is waiting for me anytime I want."

"But Brady seems to like it here," said Hailey, studying him. He seemed much more content than when they'd first met.

"That's another reason I'm anxious to work something out with Mac. At the very least, I want to establish a relationship with Mac that will allow Brady to be with his father from time to time."

"And what about the baby?"

"For her too," Linnie said. "Mac has acknowledged that he's her father, but he still wonders if I did it on purpose." An anguished expression crossed Linnie's face. "He knows I would never do anything that low. I haven't been with another man since I divorced Mac. I wouldn't do that to Brady." Her eyes filled. "The thing is, I don't want to be with anyone else."

Hailey knew how she felt. Her commitment to Nick was one she'd never break. More than a spoken vow, she couldn't imagine being with anyone else for as long as she lived. When she'd chatted with her sister, Jo, about it, Jo had agreed love could be like that.

"Before we settle on my babysitting sometime in the future, I want you to see my house and meet Zeke. If Brady and he don't get along, I won't be able to do this for you," said Hailey. Dogs could tell a lot about people from meeting them.

"Okay. That's a smart idea. That way, when anything comes up, he'll be comfortable about it," said Linnie. She turned to Brady. "Hey, buddy, we're going to visit Ms. Hailey's house. Okay?"

He glanced at Hailey and slowly nodded.

They packed up their things, left the restaurant, and went back to the parking lot at the library. "Follow me," said Hailey. "The small cove where my house sits is right off Gulf Boulevard not too far from here."

When they went to their cars, Hailey noticed the one Linnie was driving had stickers on the back indicating it was a rental.

She climbed into her SUV wondering if she was making a mistake in helping Linnie. But the fact that Linnie had volunteered she was a foster kid meant a lot. Most people she knew who'd been in the system kept it pretty quiet. And when they did talk about it, there was a sadness they couldn't hide.

Hailey kept checking the rearview mirror to make sure Linnie was following and finally turned into the driveway of her home—a sprawling one-story, tan-stucco home with a walled-in yard near the beach. A small building that their real estate agent had called a casita sat apart from the house in a corner of the yard and served as Hailey's studio. It was one of the reasons they'd bought the property.

Linnie pulled up her car next to Hailey's and helped Brady out of his car seat. He stood on the driveway gazing about him with curiosity.

Hailey went over to him. "This is where I live."

Linnie took hold of his hand. "If we're lucky, you might get to stay here for a sleepover someday."

Brady looked from his mother to Hailey and bobbed his head.

Hearing Zeke's excited barks, Hailey led them to the front door and unlocked it. As she opened the door, Zeke noticed the visitors. Barking, he ran toward Brady.

Brady's eyes widened, and then a broad smile crossed his face. "It's Zeke from the book!"

Zeke wiggled his body with excitement and then rolled over for a tummy rub.

Without hesitation, Brady knelt on the ground beside Zeke and stroked his tummy.

"Amazing!" said Linnie. "He's never acted this way with a dog before." She bent over and rubbed Zeke's head.

Zeke's tail wagged harder, and then he got on his feet and ran over to Hailey for her attention.

Laughing, Hailey picked him up. "New friends, huh?"

He licked her face and wiggled to get down.

Hailey set him down and turned to Brady and Linnie with a smile that came from deep inside her. Zeke was as perceptive a judge of people as anyone she knew. Maybe even better. And both Brady and Linnie had met his test.

"C'mon, inside. I'll show you around, so Brady can get comfortable with the idea."

Linnie and Brady followed her inside.

At the sound of soft crying, Hailey faced them and saw that Linnie was holding her face in her hands.

"What's wrong?" Hailey asked, alarmed.

Linnie looked up and dabbed at her eyes with a tissue. "I can't believe that someone like you would help me with a problem that has nothing to do with you, but I honestly didn't know who else I felt Brady and I could trust."

Hailey went over to her and hugged her awkwardly with the baby bump very evident. "Just think of it as one foster kid helping another. We've both come a long way from those times."

"You're one of the nicest women I've ever met," said Linnie, looking as if she might cry again.

"Why don't we show Brady around?" said Hailey calmly, though she understood Linnie's behavior. Growing up without support, it was sometimes difficult to accept help.

Brady let go of Linnie's hand and took hold of Hailey's.

Hailey gave him a reassuring smile. "C'mon, Brady. Let's see what you think of the place."

It didn't take long for her to be convinced that Brady and Zeke had formed a bond and that Brady was comfortable in the house.

She and Linnie chatted about living at the shore, exchanged phone numbers and addresses, and then Linnie took Brady and left.

Later, when Hailey told Nick about the promise she'd made, she explained to him that this was a special circumstance.

"After Linnie left, I researched Mac MacGrath online and saw plenty of pictures of him with Linnie and later, with both Linnie and Brady. I read the whole story about his troubles and how he was now sober. I'm hopeful that with our help, they can somehow become a family again, especially with the new baby. And when I researched Linnie online, all I could find was information about the time she was Mac's wife and when she divorced him. Nothing bad. As one foster kid to another, I want to help her. I think you'd feel the same way."

Nick wrapped his arms around her. "You're probably right."

CHAPTER 5

T he next day, Hailey walked the beach lost in thought about her new friend and the problems she faced. She was aware that having grown up in foster care, Linnie had a strength that many women her age hadn't acquired. Hailey also knew that no matter what happened, Linnie would be all right. Brady, on the other hand, had obviously been hurt by the trauma and uncertainty in his life. It was for that reason Hailey would help them out. She knew what a difference it could make. If Maddie Kirby hadn't entered her life, she might be in a different situation right now. Satisfied with her decision, Hailey headed back to the house to work on a new painting.

The days flew by as Hailey immersed herself in the book. She debated whether to opt out of storytime at the library and decided it wouldn't be fair to the kids.

When she arrived at the library, the children's area was already packed with kids, making her glad that she'd decided to come. She looked for Brady but didn't see him. Linnie was probably running a little late.

When Linnie and Brady still hadn't shown up as she finished reading to the kids, Hailey began to worry. She checked her watch. She and Linnie had planned to have coffee together afterward. Hailey was just about to call Linnie when her cell phone chimed. *Linnie.*

"Hi, Linnie! I was beginning to worry about you," she said.

"Hailey! I need your help! Can you come and pick up Brady? My water broke, and I need to get to the hospital." Linnie's voice quavered. "I'm supposed to go right away because my delivery with Brady was so quick."

"I'm on my way," said Hailey. She grabbed her purse as she clicked off the call. Linnie was usually very calm.

Heart pounding, Hailey weaved her way in and out of traffic as she drove to Linnie's rental in the North Kenwood neighborhood and found the correct building with Linnie's car parked in front.

She got out of her car and hurried to Linnie's front door. The doorbell she pressed didn't work, so she pounded on the door.

A few seconds later, she heard someone fumbling with the lock, and then the door opened a crack. A portion of Brady's face stared at her.

"Hi, Brady. I'm here to see your mom. Is she here?"

Brady flung open the door and hurried into her arms. "Something's wrong with Mommy."

Hailey rushed inside, called out to Linnie, and followed Linnie's voice to the bathroom.

"Oh, my word!" said Hailey. "You're having the baby here?" She turned to Brady. "Better go have a seat in the living room. I'll come talk to you in a minute."

Linnie was lying on the rug in the bathroom, her dress above her waist and her panties off. Tears rolled down her cheeks. "Thank God you're here! This baby isn't going to wait!"

"I'm calling 911 now," said Hailey. Her fingers shook as she punched in the number. "Help please," she said to the operator. "My friend is having a baby in her home, and we need medical help." Hailey's voice shook as she relayed how many minutes apart the pains were coming, whether the baby's head was showing, and other data the operator kept asking her while they waited for EMTs to show up.

The whole time Hailey was talking, she was aware of the moans of pain coming from Linnie. Still on the phone, Hailey went to Brady in the living room and said, "Rest here. Some medical people will be arriving soon. Let me know when they knock on the door. I'm going to stay with your mom."

He nodded solemnly, and then his eyes filled with tears.

Hailey knelt beside him and put an arm around him. "Everything's okay. Your mom is all right. She's having the baby. Soon your baby sister will be here." She hugged him and dashed back to Linnie.

"EMTs are on the way. What can I do to help you?"

Linnie grimaced as another pain struck. "Hold my hand, will you?"

Hailey took hold of Linnie's hand and cried out as Linnie squeezed her fingers so tightly she wondered if they were broken.

"Sorry," said Linnie. "Oh, oh. Here comes another pain."

"Hold on until the EMTs get here," said Hailey. "They should be here any minute."

"I can't stop. Grab some towels."

Hailey felt the room spin. She'd seen such scenes on television and in movies, but the real thing was frightening.

Just then, Brady came running into the room. "The people are here."

"Bring them here and then go back to the living room,"

said Hailey. She spread a towel beneath her, wanting something soft for the baby to land on.

A man and a woman entered the bathroom. In seconds, they took Linnie's blood pressure, checked the progress of the birth, and prepared to help with the baby's arrival.

"You're doing a great job, mom," said the woman. "We just need you to push. The baby's crowning."

Linnie glanced around. "Hailey?"

Hailey took hold of Linnie's hand. "You can do this. She's almost here."

The male EMT wiped the sweat from Linnie's forehead. "You've had quite a workout, but you're almost there."

Linnie grunted and pushed as hard as she could.

"Keep going," said the female EMT. "Keep pushing."

Watching Linnie, Hailey felt perspiration drip down her back. The humidity and closeness to others, along with the nervous excitement of the moment, filled her with tension.

With one last cry, Linnie pushed the baby out and into the waiting arms of the female EMT.

"Look, mom," the woman said. "You have a beautiful baby girl." She held up the squalling baby and handed her to Linnie to keep her warm.

Linnie and Hailey exchanged looks of wonder, and then they both began to cry.

The EMT wrapped a soft towel around the baby and said, "As soon as we get her cleaned up a bit and take care of mom, bring big brother in to see her. Then we'll take both mom and baby to the hospital to be checked out."

"Where's Brady?" said Linnie. "Poor guy was scared out of his wits, but there was nothing I could do about it but try to explain."

"I'll stay with him," Hailey said, wiping her eyes. People talked about the miracle of birth. But after seeing it firsthand, she thought of it as a religious experience.

Hailey left, went into the living room, and sat with Brady on the couch.

"Is Mommy okay?" he asked.

Hailey's smile was genuine as she hugged him to her. "She's fine. She did an excellent job having your baby sister. Wait until you see her! She's beautiful." She squeezed him. "I know you're going to be a great big brother to her."

Brady gave her a solemn look. "I'm going to tell her about Charlie and Zeke."

Hailey chuckled. "And much more, I'm sure. Oh, Brady, you're such a sweet boy."

He leaned his head against her. Hailey inhaled the "little boy" smell about him and hoped she'd have children of her own. A boy and a girl, maybe.

When the EMTs suggested that Brady come and see his baby sister, Hailey led him into the bedroom, where Linnie lay on top of a portable gurney with the baby in her arms.

"Hi, Brady. Want to see your baby sister?" Linnie said to him.

"Are you okay?" he asked.

"Yes, I am. I'm sure it was frightening to see me like that, but it's very natural. I'm healthy and happy, and so is your new sister." She opened the towel around the baby so Brady could see her. "She's perfect. Ten fingers, ten toes."

"What's her name?" Hailey asked Linnie.

"I've been privately calling her Luna, but I think it's only appropriate to include your name. How about Luna Lee?"

"Oh ... that's beautiful," Hailey said. "Thank you!" She lifted her phone and took a couple of pictures so she could always treasure this moment.

"Thank you, Hailey, for being such a dear friend," said Linnie giving her a direct look. "I don't know what I would've done if you hadn't come along. Brady and I are both grateful to you."

"Ready to go?" asked the male EMT.

"Brady can stay with me until you're ready to come home."

"That would be very helpful." Linnie wrapped an arm around Brady, pulled him close, and kissed him on the cheek. "Want to do an overnight with Hailey and Zeke?"

Brady smiled and nodded.

"Okay. That's set then. My car keys with the key to the apartment are on the kitchen counter. You'll have to move Brady's car seat from my car to yours. I'll let you know when I'm ready to come home." Linnie's eyes filled. "Thank you for everything, Hailey."

"I'm glad I was here to help. Luna Lee is a beautiful baby." With her light red hair and dark blue eyes. Luna was truly a lovely newborn.

After the EMTs left with Linnie and the baby, Hailey checked the bathroom to make sure it was clean. She noticed Linnie had set up a nursery in what must have served someone as an office. Empty bookcases and a filing cabinet lined one wall, but there was plenty of room for a crib, a changing table and other equipment suited for a baby girl. A new car seat still in the box sat on the floor.

She and Brady went into his bedroom and picked out some clothes and a toy for Brady to take with him, and then they left.

Hailey pulled her car into the garage and was pleased to see that Nick's truck was already there. She was anxious for him to meet Brady and was pleased they'd have some time together.

When they walked into the kitchen, Zeke made a beeline for Brady. Grinning, Brady knelt on the floor and laughed when Zeke crawled into his lap and licked his face.

Nick walked into the room. "Who do we have here?" he asked, staring at the scene in front of him.

"Nick, I want you to meet Brady. He's going to spend the night with us while his mother recovers from having her baby girl at home." She glanced at Brady. "Linnie did a great job, and now Brady is a big brother."

Brady's lips curved with pride.

"I'll tell you all about it later," said Hailey. "She's a beautiful baby. Linnie has named her Luna Lee. The Lee is because I was there to help her."

Nick's eyes widened with the news. He smiled at Brady. "Hi, Brady. I'm Nick. Zeke and I are happy you've come to visit."

Brady's gaze settled on Nick.

Hailey held her breath as they studied one another.

"Zeke and I are friends," said Brady. "Just like Charlie and Zeke in the books we read."

"Zeke can tell you're someone special," said Nick. "I hope you brought a bathing suit."

Brady turned to Hailey.

"I packed one for you," she said. "The pool is heated, and I thought you might like to go swimming with us." She waited for Brady to say something. Maybe he didn't like the water.

After a moment, Brady said, "Okay. Mac likes to swim too."

Hailey and Nick exchanged meaningful looks.

"Let me show you to your room. Do you remember where it is?"

Brady nodded, got up, and headed down the hallway to one of the guest rooms. On his earlier visit, he'd chosen the one closest to the kitchen. Zeke followed at his heels.

Nick laughed. "Guess he's feeling right at home."

"I hope so," said Hailey. "This is unexpected, but between

the connection I've developed with him and Zeke's enthusiasm, I'm hoping we remain special friends to him."

Hailey carried the canvas bag with Brady's things to the guest room. He was sitting on the bed with Zeke.

Hailey went over to them. "We have to lift Zeke onto the bed and back down to the floor, so he doesn't hurt his back. Okay?"

"He cried to get up. I lifted him," said Brady.

"That's good," Hailey said. She pulled his trunks out of the bag and handed it to him. "Can you get dressed by yourself?"

"Yes. Mommy says I'm a big boy."

"You are. When you're in your trunks, come back to the kitchen. Nick and I will meet you there. Do not go outside to the pool unless one of us is with you. That's the number one rule here. All right?"

"Okay."

"I'll wait for you in the kitchen." Hailey left him, pleased by how he relaxed was in their home. Perhaps he and Linnie had lived in a house of a similar size. Or maybe he sensed the love she and Nick shared. Either way, Hailey was relieved, even if his stay was just overnight.

Nick was waiting for her in the kitchen dressed for a swim. "Brady's a cute kid and seems right at home. I thought you said he was shy and didn't talk much."

"He normally is much shyer. I think Zeke's presence makes a big difference. That, and the fact that since coming to the library, he's talking more and more."

"So, tell me what went on. His mother had the baby at home?"

"Yes. It's a good thing I showed up when I did. When Linnie and Brady didn't appear at the library for storytime, I was worried. Then Linnie called and asked me to come get Brady because her water had broken. Apparently, she had an unusually fast delivery with Brady and knew she needed to get to the hospital right away. But when I got to her house, it was too late. The baby wasn't waiting for anyone. My heart almost stopped when I saw what was happening. I called 911. They sent EMTs to the apartment." Hailey's eyes filled. "It was such a miracle to see the baby appear and begin to cry. I hope that will happen for us one day, though I'd definitely choose to be in the hospital."

He pulled her to him. "That day will come. And when it does, you'll be fine. I know you. Beneath all your gentle ways lies a lioness."

She chuckled. She did feel that way sometimes, especially when she saw someone else hurting.

"I'm ready," said Brady. He appeared wearing his trunks over his underpants.

Hailey decided to say nothing about it. She'd brought extra clothing for him.

"Go ahead, you two. I'll bring towels for all of us." Hailey left them to change her clothes, wishing she could stay to see their interaction.

A few minutes later, when she walked outside, Brady was sitting on a step in the shallow end kicking his feet happily. Nick was standing nearby, rubbing Zeke's ears.

"How's the water?" Hailey asked.

"Nice and warm. Now that you're here, I'll do a few laps," said Nick. "Brady was waiting for you before getting into the water all the way."

"Okay, I'll sit with you for a while, Brady, and when you're ready, let me know if you want to go to deeper water. If you come for another visit, we'll be sure to have some toys for you."

While they sat, Zeke lowered himself on the pool deck between them, keeping watch at their shoulder level.

After a while, Hailey said, "I'll hold your hands if you want to try to get in the water all the way."

Brady grinned and took hold of her hands.

Hailey walked away from the steps with him hanging onto her. Then he began to kick and splash as if it was part of a routine he knew. Probably something he did with his mother.

Later, sitting on the edge of the pool with towels wrapped around them, she tried to get Brady to tell her and Nick a little more about his life with his mother, but he turned quiet.

"Is everyone hungry?" said Nick rising to his feet. "I'm going to start the grill. Hope you like hamburgers, Brady."

Brady grinned. "I do."

They went inside to change their clothes.

Hailey took a moment to call Linnie. "How are you doing?"

"The baby and I are fine. They checked her over, and she seems to have handled everything well. She's passed all their tests with excellent results. They'll let us go home tomorrow."

"Do you want visitors? I thought maybe Brady would like to see you and his sister before settling down for the night."

"That would be lovely. Can you bring me a change of clothes and the baby's car seat? Also, I didn't have time to grab Luna's outfit for the hospital. It's sitting on top of the bureau."

"Sure. Tell me what you need, and I'll bring it. Is seven-thirty okay for a visit?" Hailey asked.

"Perfect. Can't wait to see you."

With all the arrangements made, Hailey ended the call. She'd worried that living away from her family would leave her very alone, but with Janna's friendship and now Linnie's, along with other acquaintances, she realized how full her life was becoming.

Brady was quiet as he ate his hamburger. But when Hailey asked him if he was ready to go visit his mother and the baby, he became more animated and dug into the ice cream she offered him.

"You two go ahead. I'll put the dishes in the dishwasher," said Nick.

Hailey gave him a grateful smile. "Thanks. We won't be gone long."

As she drove to the rental to pick up the items Linnie had requested, Hailey kept conversation with Brady alive by talking about some of his favorite things. She'd already learned he liked hamburgers and ice cream. As they spoke, Hailey remembered the stuffed dog she'd bought one of her nieces and decided that would be a great way to help Brady get comfortable before going to bed.

Hailey unlocked the door to the house with the keys she'd found on the kitchen counter earlier and stepped inside. The small, sparsely furnished house was immaculate. Observing this well-tended home, Hailey was more certain than ever that helping Linnie was the right thing to do, especially if it meant bringing a family together.

She packed Linnie's things in a plastic bag, picked up the car seat and outfit for Luna, and helped Brady choose a toy to bring with him. Then they headed for the hospital.

"Are you excited to see your baby sister?" Hailey asked Brady as she led him into the maternity area.

"Yes. She's a baby. I'm a big boy."

Still smiling, Hailey let go of his hand. "Okay, here we are. Better go say hi to your mom."

Brady raced through the open doorway. "Hi, Mom!"

"Oh, Brady, come here and give me a giant hug. You were a very brave boy today."

Hailey's vision blurred as she observed them. Brady was such a special child.

Linnie looked up at her. "How are things going?"

"Great," Hailey answered. "It's been fun."

Luna's cries circled them.

Hailey and Brady stood by as Linnie lifted the baby onto the bed with her. "Look how much red her hair has," said Linnie. "She gets that from her father."

"Does he know?" Hailey asked.

Linnie's beaming smile filled her face. "Yes. We're going to meet in a week or so to talk. He seems pretty excited about it. We'd like to get things resolved before Christmas. We're talking about getting back together again."

"Sounds great," said Hailey, leaning over to get a better look at the baby. "She's beautiful."

"Can I touch her?" asked Brady, his voice filled with awe.

"Go ahead, but gently," said Linnie.

Brady gingerly touched Luna's head. The baby's eyes seemed to focus on Brady for a moment.

"I'm your big brother," said Brady, taking hold of one of her hands.

When Luna began to cry, Brady patted her shoulder. "It's all right, baby sister. I'm here."

Hailey and Linnie glanced at one another, sharing this emotional moment.

Linnie took hold of Brady's hand and smiled at him. "I'm proud of you, Brady. I know I can always trust you to help take care of your sister."

He bobbed his head proudly.

Luna's cries this time were not going to stop without being fed. Linnie undid the tie of her gown and lifted the baby to her breast.

"We won't keep you," said Hailey. "What time should I plan on picking you up in the morning?"

"I'd think pretty early. I'll give you a call." Linnie kissed Brady. "Goodnight, son. See you in the morning. Behave for Hailey."

"I will," he answered solemnly.

As they left the room, Hailey said to Brady, "I'm proud of

you too. You've handled the situation very well. You're a nice guest and a great big brother."

Though he didn't say anything, her words brought a satisfied smile to his face.

At home, the day's activities seemed to catch up with Brady. He had no problem with it being bedtime. After she'd helped him put on his pajamas and brush his teeth, Hailey said, "I have a special gift for you."

"For me?" Brady's eyes sparkled with excitement.

"Yes. When I was a young girl, not too much older than you, my new mother gave me a stuffed dog that one of my new sisters called Charlie. Every time I wasn't sure about things, Charlie helped me through them. That's where the idea for the Charlie and Zeke stories came from." Hailey handed him the stuffed tan dog with floppy ears. "This one's for you."

Brady hugged it to him. "He's soft like Zeke."

"Do you want to name him?" Hailey asked.

Brady thought for a moment. "I'll call him Charlie. Now I have Charlie here and Zeke there." He pointed to Zeke, who was staring up at them with pleading eyes, waiting to be picked up.

"Okay. I'll let Zeke stay with you for a little bit. Chances are when you wake up, he'll be gone. But you two can cuddle until you fall asleep." She lifted Zeke onto the bed. "I'll come back and check on you in a little while. 'Night." Hailey leaned over and kissed him on the cheek, hoping she wasn't crossing a line with him.

They gazed at one another for a moment, and then Hailey left the room.

Later, after she'd retrieved Zeke and climbed into bed with Nick, Hailey let out a long sigh. Today had held one surprise after another. It had also filled her mind about a book with Charlie acting as a big brother to a baby sister. Brady and Luna had been precious together.

She turned and faced Nick. "Thanks for being helpful with Brady. He seems comfortable with you."

"He's a great kid. The family has some things to work out —things that aren't any of our business." He cupped her face in his broad hands. "I understand you want everyone you know to be happy, but it doesn't always work out that way. I love that you care; I just don't want you to get hurt."

"I know." She reached for him, and when his lips met hers, she sighed with happiness.

CHAPTER 6

The next morning, Hailey was startled by Zeke's barks as he leapt off the bed. She sat up groggily and saw Brady standing in the doorway holding his dog, Charlie.

"Hi, Brady. Did you have a nice sleep?"

He nodded sleepily.

Hailey climbed out of bed careful not to disturb Nick, who was snoring softly. She grabbed her silk robe, slid it on over her shorty pajamas, and went over to him.

"Let's put Zeke outside and get something to eat. Shall we?"

Brady took her hand.

In the kitchen, while Zeke was outside, Hailey sat at the kitchen table with Brady.

"Do I see Mommy today?" he asked.

"Sure. We'll pick up your mom and the baby at the hospital and take them home. But first, we'll do some grocery shopping."

"For Luna?"

"For you and Mommy. Luna's so little that all she has is milk."

Brady grew serious. "I'm big. She's little. But I'll take care of her."

Hailey smiled at his earnestness. "You're already a good big brother. Now, let's get you some breakfast and me some coffee."

"I want mixed-up eggs," said Brady.

Hailey laughed. "Do you mean scrambled eggs?"

"Uh, huh, but Mommy and I call them mixed-up," said Brady.

"Fair enough. Do you want toast too?" she asked.

"With cinn-ma-mom sugar."

His words made her smile. "All right. How about some juice while you wait?"

"Okay."

Hailey poured him a glass of orange juice and was mixing up the eggs as Brady liked to think of it when Nick walked into the room.

"Ah, good morning, everyone." He tousled Brady's hair and gave Hailey a kiss.

Zeke barked for attention.

Chuckling, Nick walked over to the cupboard, retrieved a doggy treat, and gave it to Zeke.

"It's a beautiful day," Hailey said. "Anyone want to go to the beach to make sandcastles?"

Brady's eyes rounded. "Me!"

Hailey loved Brady's enthusiasm and couldn't wait to show him one of her favorite things to do. As always, she'd tuck away any ideas that came to her while working with him for future material.

After breakfast, Hailey checked in with Linnie, learned she wouldn't be discharged until after lunch, and got herself and Brady ready for the beach. Nick promised to join them after he took care of a phone call to the school.

As they walked across the sand, Hailey pointed to a cattle egret walking along the beach in front of them. Zeke ran ahead, barking, and the white egret lifted into the sky, its long orange legs trailing behind.

"That's a big bird with long legs. I've seen it in a book," said Brady. "Mommy reads it to me."

Hailey was pleased. She'd already painted an egret for her seashore book.

"Shall we look for bird footprints in the sand?" she asked.

"Yes!" said Brady. He lifted his bare foot from the sand and kicked up a bunch. "Those are mine."

Hailey laughed out loud. "I guess you could say so. C'mon with me." She led him onto the hard-packed sand at the water's edge. Sandpipers and other shorebirds raced along the frothy edge of the water ahead of them, leaving prints in the wet sand behind them.

"I see one," said Brady. "One, two, three, four, twenty, one hundred, a thousand," he cried with enthusiasm.

Hailey grinned at him. "There are a lot of them. Careful where you're walking. Some of the shells are broken and could cut your feet."

Brady stayed at the water's edge, and then he faced the Gulf to watch the seagulls swirl above them, their cries shattering the early morning air. When he turned to her, he studied her and said softly, "I like you."

Touched, Hailey smiled and took hold of his hand. "I like you, too. Shall we build a castle now?"

He nodded with excitement.

Hailey set down the towels and canvas bag holding the shovels and pails they needed, along with bottles of water and a bag of snacks for later.

On the flat wet area of sand not far from the water's edge, she made a circle in the sand. "We'll build the castle in the middle." She'd learned to give herself enough space for flexibility.

"Here." Hailey handed Brady a bucket. "Let's fill that up with sand almost to the top. Then we'll add water, letting it soak through the sand before turning the bucket upside down."

Brady proudly carried his bucket to drier sand, where Hailey helped him fill the bucket.

After Hailey wet down the sand inside, they dumped it in the middle of the circle together.

Brady clapped his hands. "It's a castle."

"Perhaps," said Hailey. "Or we could make it bigger. What do you think?"

"Bigger," said Brady, and they grinned at one another.

After they'd dumped three buckets of wet sand, Hailey checked her watch and realized they wouldn't have time to finish the castle.

"We have to get ready to pick up Mommy and Luna soon. Before then, we need to run a few errands. I'm sorry, we can't finish this one. But we'll make another castle another day."

Brady's lower lip jutted out and then disappeared. "Promise?"

She raised her hand. "I promise."

They went back to the house, washed up, gathered Brady's things, including Charlie Dog, and then headed to the grocery store. Hailey wanted to make sure Linnie wouldn't have any need to leave the house for the next couple of days.

At the store, Brady helped pick out some fruit, cereal, milk, juice, and some easy pre-prepared meals. Just before they reached the check-out lane, they found a display of stuffed animals.

"Can we get one for Luna?" he asked.

"Sure. You choose the one you want for her," Hailey said, touched by his thoughtfulness.

Brady searched through the huge basket holding the toys and lifted a pink lamb from the pile. "I want this one for her."

"It's a lovely lamb," said Hailey. "You can give it to her when we pick her up."

"What should I call the lamb?" asked Brady looking very serious.

Hailey knelt by him and looked him in the eyes. "What do you think? Lambs are fuzzy, have curly coats, say b-a-a-a, and love to play around."

Brady's face lit with excitement. "Let's call her Fuzzy."

"That sounds like the perfect name for her. The lamb has a lot of pink fuzz."

"What a cute little boy," said an older woman passing them.

"Thank you," said Hailey, even though she could take no credit for him. But Linnie could. She'd be sure to tell her.

They went to Linnie's house, got things in order there, and headed for the hospital.

Brady sat in the car seat Hailey had installed in the back-seat of her car. Holding the lamb in his arms, he was as cute as the woman in the grocery store had proclaimed.

Hailey parked the car, phoned Linnie, and took Brady inside to the maternity area.

When they got to Linnie's room, she was dressed and sitting on the edge of the bed. The baby was lying on the bed beside her on a green swaddling cloth. She was dressed in the darling little onesie Hailey had brought in the evening before. A green knit cap covered her scalp.

"Hi, Brady," cried, Linnie. "I missed you so much! Come see your baby sister."

Brady lifted the pink lamb. "I got this for her. I call her Fuzzy."

"How sweet! Give me a kiss, then you can show it to her."

Brady ran over to Linnie and into her arms.

Watching them and seeing the baby, Hailey reminded herself that her time would come. Though she and Nick no longer discussed it, they were still trying hard to make it happen.

A nurse rolled a wheelchair into the room. "Are we ready to go home?"

"Yes," said Brady. "Can I ride in that?"

"That's for your mother," said the nurse kindly.

Linnie beamed at her. "Hailey, will you help the nurse get Luna into her car seat?"

"Sure," said Hailey, glad to be useful.

As soon as Linnie was situated in the wheelchair, the nurse handed Hailey the car seat with the baby strapped inside. "She sure is an adorable little thing."

Hailey looked down at the perfect little face staring up at her. A wisp of light, reddish-brown hair peeked out from under her cap. Hailey's eyes stung with tears.

"Coming?" Linnie asked, turning and calling to her from the wheelchair.

"Oh yes. I'm right behind you," said Hailey, shaking off her emotion.

When they got to the entrance to the hospital, Hailey handed the baby in her car seat to the nurse and left to get her vehicle.

When she pulled up to where Linnie and the others waited for her, Linnie's excitement was clear.

The nurse helped Linnie into the front seat and then worked with Hailey to see that the car seat holding Luna was properly installed in the back near the one for Brady.

"Ready?" Hailey asked, and at a nod from the nurse, she got behind the wheel and slowly drove away with her precious cargo.

When everything was in order at the house, and both car seats were taken out of her car, Hailey asked Linnie if she should stay.

"Thanks. I appreciate everything you've done, but I need to learn to handle this myself."

"Okay. Call if you change your mind." Hailey said goodbye and drove to her house. She needed a long walk on the beach to settle her emotions before Nick got home. She didn't want him to see how upset she was about not getting pregnant. She didn't know why it hadn't happened, and she had no family history to help her.

At home, Zeke raced to greet her. She lifted him into her arms and held him a little too long. For now, he was her baby. "How about a walk on the beach?"

He barked and wagged his tail and then squirmed with excitement as she tried to put his harness on.

As they stepped onto the sand, Hailey paused. Her disappointment squeezed her insides and then lessened as she headed for the water. The timeless movement of the Gulf waters eased her mind of the worry and longing that had made her weepy. *Time would take care of things*, she reminded herself and headed down the beach. The earlier sun had disappeared behind the thick gray clouds that now covered the sky. A breeze holding the distinct smell of forthcoming rain was cool against her face.

"Let's run," she said to Zeke, and set off along the water's edge, needing to fill her lungs with the fresh air of hope.

Over the next couple of days, Hailey called Linnie to offer help or popped in to surprise her.

"Thank goodness, you're here," said Linnie one morning. "I need to take a shower and wash my hair. Will you read to Brady while I do that? If Luna wakes, I have a bottle all ready for her."

"Sure," said Hailey, hoping for some private time with Brady.

Just as she and Brady finished reading the first page of a book, Luna woke.

"Give me time to make sure the baby's bottle is warm enough, and then I'll read the rest of the story with you while I feed Luna."

Brady's lower lip jutted out, but he nodded.

A few minutes later, as she was feeding the baby, Luna filled her diaper.

"Eeyuw!" cried Brady, getting up. "I don't want to read anymore."

Linnie appeared, her hair dripping wet. "Oh, oh. Time for a diaper change. Brady, want to show Ms. Hailey where we keep the diapers? I'll change the baby."

Brady ran off, and Linnie faced Hailey with a smile. "Thanks for helping. You don't know how much it means. I can take over from here."

"Are you sure?" Hailey asked.

"Yes. I don't want to scare you off. I appreciate all the time you've given us. But I've got to get used to doing this on my own."

"Call me anytime," said Hailey. "It's good practice for me."

Linnie gave her a quick hug. "Don't worry. Your time will come."

Hailey smiled and secretly crossed her fingers.

I'm
ren't
don't

she is
Luna.
o take

CHAPTER 7

F or the next couple of weeks, even though she checked in with Linnie from time to time, Hailey concentrated on Christmas. To her delight, Janna, Mike, and his daughter, Zoey, agreed to come for Christmas brunch. Janna had shared numerous conversations with her about the way she and Mike were quickly bonding. Hailey was thrilled for her.

On this Tuesday morning, with just two days until Christmas, Hailey was surprised by a phone call from Linnie.

"'Morning," Hailey said. "How's everything at your house?"

"Better than ever." Linnie's voice rang with happiness. "Luna is an easy baby. Brady has been amazing with her. Best of all, Mac and I have been talking a lot lately, discussing getting back together. He wants to meet me in Naples."

"That's very exciting. I'm pleased for all of you."

Linnie sighed. "Me too. There's only one problem. We've agreed he doesn't get to see the children until we've settled everything. I can't disappoint Brady all over again. Mac understands and wants to make it right for both the kids. Oh, Hailey, he's the man I've always loved."

"That's fabulous. How can I help?"

"Would you … I mean, could you … the kids need a place to stay tonight."

Hailey thought of Brady, and before she could stop herself, she blurted, "You want me to take the kids overnight? Sure, I can do that."

"It won't be for too long. I'll return tomorrow morning. I know you probably have plans for Christmas. Having the kids won't interfere with that, will it? After reading the Charlie books about Christmas, I know how much you love that holiday."

"No, the timing should be fine if you're back tomorrow morning, as you've said. In fact, you and the kids are welcome for Christmas brunch, if you can make it."

"That's just it. If this goes as we want, Mac and I and the kids will spend the holiday together in Miami. But thanks for all you've done for us and for agreeing to take the kids. I told Mac about you, and he can't wait to meet you. Something about foster kids sticking together, you know?"

Hailey felt her lips curve. She'd always volunteered whenever she could to help foster kids. This was simply another example.

"I'm sure it'll be all right with Nick. Brady is already comfortable here. What do I need to do at this end to take care of the baby?"

"I'll bring plenty of bottles, equipment, diapers, and cloth-ng, and all the stuff she needs. She should continue to sleep t of the time. I've got a new portable little bed for her that ld be easy for you to use. If you want, you can come here I'll go over everything with you again. Then you might ore comfortable."

hanks, but after being around Brady and Luna, I'm well acquainted with their routines."

s, your help has been great. Luna still wakes up for a during the night, and she gets up early. I wish I could make that part easier for you, but it's out of my hands. Are you sure you're willing to do this?

Hailey hesitated. She hadn't spoken to Nick yet. But then she thought of all the possibilities for Brady, Linnie, and the baby. "Yes. You go. We'll be fine. It's just overnight. I can handle it."

"I'll be sure to have us both sign a medical release, just in case you might ever need it."

A ping of worry hit Hailey's insides. Nothing like that could go wrong, could it?

Hailey was surprised by Nick's wariness when she told him about the arrangement with Brady and the baby.

"This is a bit overboard for Linnie to ask this of you, don't you think? A two-week-old baby and a four-year-old?"

Hailey studied Nick. He was a kind, generous man. She understood his concern, but this was special. Very special.

Nick gave her a steady look. "I'm afraid you're getting too involved, and I don't want you to get hurt, that's all. We'll help this time, but I hope it doesn't become a habit."

"This one favor of mine can affect four lives in an everlasting, joyful way," Hailey said, believing it with all her heart. "The fact that Mac and Linnie are both foster kids means even more to me. Don't worry. I'll get up with the baby and try to keep her quiet during the night so you can sleep."

"Aw, Hailey, you know that's not why I'm upset. worried that you're doing this in part because you a pregnant yet. Another thing that concerns me is that we know Linnie that well and we've never met Mac."

"You will soon. Linnie is a good mother. I see how with Brady and for a short time, how she's been with That speaks more to me than anything. I'm not going back my word."

When Nick's arms wrapped around her, Hailey felt better. She and Nick didn't argue much because they understood one another. In this case, there was no going back. She'd made a promise to Linnie and she'd keep it.

"I love you, Hailey," said Nick, nuzzling her neck. "Let's not disagree. We'll work together to take care of Brady and Luna. It'll be practice for us."

"We've always talked about five children. Maybe after we do this, we'll think smaller."

Nick chuckled. "It doesn't mean we won't continue trying for many more than that. Practice makes perfect."

She laughed and stood on her toes to kiss him.

Later, when she and Nick greeted Linnie and Brady and they helped bring the baby equipment in from the car, Hailey wondered if she'd been foolish after all. What did she know about being a mother? Maybe not as much as she'd thought.

Linnie helped Hailey set up the portable bed, showed her how to mix formula for a bottle, demonstrated how the newborn disposable diapers worked best, and told her about the various lotions to use. It all made sense to Hailey, but she took careful notes anyway.

"One last thing," said Linnie, pulling a paper out of her purse. "I want you to co-sign this, so there are no issues if you should need to take either kid to the doctors or worse."

Hailey looked at the document Linnie handed her. It seemed pretty straightforward about permission to act in Linnie's place should either child need medical attention. Her eyes stopped at the last paragraph. "What's this?"

"My neighbor suggested I add this, just as a precaution, and make two copies. She's the nervous type. I wasn't going to do it, but then decided I'd better. I know I worry too much. Maybe it's my new mom hormones or the fact that I was in the foster care system. But I agree with her. This is important. It makes you and Nick guardians of the kids should I be unavailable for any reason. I suppose that means if I'm in a hospital somewhere." She gave Hailey a teasing grin. "Of if Mac and I decide to take off."

Horror filled Hailey at the thought. "Don't ever tease me like that again."

Linnie reached out, touched Hailey's shoulder, and gave her a steady look. "You know I would never leave my children. And I'm pretty safe in thinking that Mac wouldn't either." A flush of color flooded her cheeks. "He's been very loving on the phone. He says since he's been out of rehab almost two years ago, he's tried to forget me, but he can't. After our last meeting, he wants to try to regain everything we've lost. He says he loves me and loves having the kids. This time, I know he means it."

Seeing the way Linnie was trying to hold back tears at the same time a smile lifted the corners of her mouth, Hailey pulled her into a hug. "I'm happy for you, Linnie."

Hailey signed the documents, kept one for herself, and handed the other to Linnie. "Yours is the type of story everyone wants to hear after the rough times you two have had."

"I know, and it couldn't come at a better time of year." She gave Hailey an encouraging smile. "Maybe this will be a rewarding time of year for you too."

Hailey returned the smile and hoped Linnie was right.

Brady sat nearby on the living room carpet holding his stuffed dog and patting Zeke, who'd turned on his back for a tummy rub.

"Come say goodbye," said Linnie, holding out her arms to him. "I'll see you tomorrow morning. Behave for Ms. Hailey, okay?"

Brady nodded and hugged his mother goodbye. "See you tomorrow. I'll take care of Luna."

Linnie laughed. "Thank you. You can help Ms. Hailey. You and Zeke and Charlie."

"And me," said Nick quietly, holding Luna in his arms.

"Oh, yes. By all means. I'm pleased to meet you," said Linnie. "I hope Luna doesn't keep you guys up tonight. She's been on a pretty consistent schedule."

"No need to worry. Hailey said she'll take care of the night feedings," said Nick, giving Hailey an exaggerated wink.

The three adults laughed together and then Linnie headed for the door. "Thanks again. See you tomorrow. I'm pretty sure Mac will be with me."

"Good luck with everything," said Hailey. "Brady and I have another castle to build."

Brady's eyes lit. "Yes. You promised."

"I can see they're in excellent hands," said Linnie laughing. "See you soon."

Once Linnie had gone, Hailey felt the weight of responsibility on her shoulders. This would be important practice for her, she thought, taking Luna from Nick and laying her down in the little portable bed they'd set up in a corner of the living room away from traffic but close enough to hear her if she stirred and cried.

"Castles! I want castles!" said Brady.

Hailey looked to Nick.

"Go ahead. I'll watch the baby while she naps. But if I signal you, come quickly."

"Okay, we'll stay right in front of the house," said Hailey, relieved Nick was being so cooperative.

That evening, after Brady had his bath and was tucked into bed with his stuffed dog and Zeke, Hailey rested on the couch with Nick.

"Luckily, it's just for one night," said Hailey. "We have to get used to this routine step by step. Not all at once."

Nick wrapped an arm around her shoulder. "I have a feeling that things are going to work out for us. A lot of it has to do with the idea that we're not talking about getting pregnant all the time."

"I agree," said Hailey. "I've spoken to the doctor. She doesn't think there's anything wrong with me. It just takes a break sometimes for things to happen."

Luna's cries lifted in the air.

Hailey and Nick faced one another.

"I thought you just fed her," said Nick.

Hailey frowned. "I did. Maybe it's a gas bubble. I'll go see." Hailey got to her feet and went to the alcove outside the master bedroom to check on Luna. Before she reached Luna, Hailey knew from the smell what the problem was.

"There, there," crooned Hailey, lifting Luna into her arms and carrying her to the guest bathroom in the hallway.

"We'll get you changed and burped, and then you can go back to sleep, shall we?"

The baby glanced at the bright light overhead and quieted, as if she knew she was in a new place. Hailey changed the baby's diaper, wrapped her in a fresh swaddle, and rubbed her back.

After a couple of healthy burps, the baby closed her eyes and Hailey tiptoed back to Luna's bed and laid her inside.

"How is she?" asked Nick when Hailey returned to the living room.

"Fine," she said. "For a few moments anyway."

"Why don't we go to bed? Who knows how often we'll be up with her?"

"First, I want to call Alissa. I've been able to talk to Stevie and Jo, but I want to wish Alissa a safe trip."

"Okay, but don't get into one of your marathon telephone

conversations," said Nick. "We only have a few hours to try and sleep."

Hailey gave him a wave and then reached for her phone. Talking to her sisters was important to her, keeping the closeness alive.

Sounding out of breath, Alissa picked up on the fifth ring.

"Hi. I hope this isn't a bad time to chat," said Hailey.

"Not at all. I'm finishing packing for tomorrow and could frankly use a pep talk. The truth is, I'm worried sick about being with Jed's parents for the holidays. I'm sure they're expecting us to come crawling back to them, ask them to accept Jed in the family business, and will think I'm a lousy mother because nothing I do is ever right."

"Alissa, you know you're a good mother. And you and Jed are so happy together. Surely, they'll see that. And when they learn how successful he's been, won't they be happy for him?"

Alissa sighed. "I wish I could be sure of that."

"Relax. His parents can't be that bad. They raised Jed to be such a great guy."

"Maybe you're right," said Alissa. "What's going on with you?"

"Remember Linnie, the woman I told you about who has the adorable little boy named Brady?"

"Oh yes. You and Brady formed a very nice relationship, and you helped her with her baby. What's happening now?"

"She and her ex are meeting in Naples as we speak. Nick and I are taking care of Brady and Luna overnight. Linnie says she and Mac have been talking about getting back together, that they love each other very much. She's sure he'll be with her when she returns tomorrow. Isn't that great?"

"If it all works out, yes. I'm surprised Nick was agreeable to having both Brady and the baby overnight. You told me he was a little wary about getting too close to the situation."

Hailey laughed. "You should see him with the kids. He's a

natural father. It makes me feel secure about our trying for kids of our own. I'd better go. Nick's already in bed."

"Wow! That's a little early. We haven't eaten yet."

"Even with the two-hour time difference, it's early. But we're pretty sure we'll both be up in the night. Thank heaven, Linnie returns tomorrow. But, like I said, this has been good for us."

"Keep up the nice work," said Alissa. "I've got a family to feed."

"Have a safe trip to Seattle. You'll be fine. Everyone loves you, Alissa."

"Everyone but Jed's mother," Alissa grumbled. "I'll call you on Christmas Day."

"Thanks. Hugs all around,"

"To you and yours as well," said Alissa, ending the call.

Hoping Alissa was wrong about her mother-in-law, Hailey headed to bed.

CHAPTER 8

Hailey stirred in her sleep, irritated by a high-pitched squeal of displeasure. Beside her, Nick snored softly.

Rubbing her eyes, Hailey sat up. Then it hit her. Baby Luna was crying, and it sounded as if it was becoming serious. She climbed out of bed and stood a moment to get her bearings before padding to the alcove. Luna was awake and had managed to get her hands out of the swaddle. Scrunching her pink face, she let out a wail and waved her tiny fists in the air.

"Oh, baby, I'll get you changed, and then you can have a bottle."

Lifting Luna in her arms, Hailey marveled at how perfect this tiny human being was. Even as Luna's voice erupted again, she was adorable.

Crooning to quiet her, Hailey changed her, then carried Luna into the kitchen to heat the bottle of formula. She'd prepared it earlier, as Linnie had instructed.

Seated at the kitchen table with the baby, Hailey yawned as Luna took her bottle. By the time the baby was finished and burped, Hailey could hardly keep her eyes open. She put

Luna back to bed, stumbled into her room, and climbed alongside Nick under the covers, hoping to get more sleep. She closed her eyes and lay there thinking of everything she'd done, hoping she'd gotten everything right. She told herself that all was in order, but her mind circled around the idea that she might have missed a step. It was one thing to have helped Linnie, but quite another to be on her own.

Hailey was sleeping hard when she heard Luna cry again. She checked the bedside clock and realized four hours had passed. She got out of bed and hurried to get the baby before she woke the others. It was bad enough that Zeke roused every time Luna cried and then decided to go outside himself.

Luna was soaking wet when Hailey found her in the little bed.

"Poor baby. We'll have to get a whole new onesie on you and make sure you're nice and clean. Stripping off the wet swaddle, onesie, and diaper, Hailey covered Luna with another blanket while she gently washed the baby's body, one tiny section at a time so she wouldn't become chilled. Linnie had left behind organic soaps, lotions, and oils.

Luna kicked and stared at Hailey. After a few minutes of being fascinated with someone new, Luna let out a wail that Hailey knew wouldn't stop until she fed her.

She was in the kitchen feeding the baby when Nick walked in. "Luna slept well, huh? How many hours has it been?"

"This isn't the first time I've been up with her," said Hailey, trying not to be annoyed by Nick's being able to sleep through Luna's earlier cries. "I'm hoping after I feed her, Luna will sleep for a long time and that her brother is a late sleeper."

"It looks like you have things under control. Guess I'll go back to bed. Thanks, Hailey."

Luna made a little noise.

Hailey looked down at her sweet face, and all irritation fled. Taking care of Luna was important practice for her.

As soon as she could, she put Luna back in her bed and headed to her own, intent on getting some sleep.

Nick stirred as she slid into bed and molded herself to him. If she slowed her breathing to match his, it helped to get back to sleep.

Hailey had no idea how long it had been when she felt something touch her face. She jerked away and found Brady standing beside the bed, staring at her. His stuffed dog was in his arms.

"Hi, Brady. What do you want? It's early."

"Can I lie down with you? Mommy lets me do that when I can't sleep."

Hailey sighed softly. "Sure. Climb up. You can sleep with Zeke between Nick and me."

Brady climbed on top of the bed and settled down between them. After receiving several kisses from Zeke, Brady quieted, and Hailey tried to sleep once more.

She was dozing when Nick got up and woke Brady and Zeke.

"Sorry," Nick whispered.

"It's okay," she responded, smiling when Brady snuggled closer and Zeke kissed her face.

They lay still for several minutes before Luna cried.

"Okay, boys, it's time for me to get up. Brady, if you want, you can stay here and rest."

"No, I want to be with you. When's Mommy coming?"

"Later this morning," Hailey said, excited about the idea of an afternoon nap. She headed out of the room to get Luna.

Nick was standing by Luna's bed, gazing down at her. "She sure is small. I've forgotten how tiny Regan was when she was born."

"She's perfect, but she's petite. I'll take care of her, and then while I take a shower and get cleaned up, maybe you'll keep an ear out for Luna and an eye on Brady."

"Sure. This has been a wake-up call for me. We have a very peaceful life. Children will certainly complicate it."

Hailey's heart stopped beating and then raced with alarm. "You're not rethinking starting a family right away, are you?"

"No. I'm just trying to tell myself how real the changes will be. We're lucky because I've saved money for years. When the time comes, we can afford to hire help for you."

Hailey lifted Luna in her arms. "That's a nice offer, Nick, but after what I went through as a child, I believe a mother should be involved with her children."

Nick wrapped an arm around her and smiled down at Luna. "Of course. Luckily, we don't have to worry about that now. Let's just get through the holidays and then we can talk more about it."

His lips came down on hers. Nick was right. They'd talk later, though they'd discussed it and had agreed on such details before.

Hailey had just finished drying her body from her shower when her cell rang. She raced into the bedroom to take the call. *Linnie.*

"Hi, how are you?" Hailey asked.

"Wonderful," Linnie said, her voice ringing with happiness. "Mac and I have decided to reunite. We're driving up to your house this morning to pick up the kids. Then we're going to pack up as much as we can from the house. The kids and I are moving to Miami with Mac."

"Really? That's fantastic! I'm so happy for all of you. Brady will be thrilled. He's been asking when you're coming back."

"Tell him we'll be there in a little while. Oh, Hailey, I can't thank you enough for taking care of the kids for me. I realize it was a lot to ask, but I knew they'd be in good hands. If they'd been with me, I don't think this reunion would've worked. Mac and I have talked and talked for hours and remembered what we had. Oh, here he is. He wants to say hi."

"Hello, Hailey. Mac MacGrath here. I just want to thank you. Linnie said your helping us has a lot to do with the three of us being foster kids, but I think it's more than that. Can't wait to meet you and Nick. Thanks for taking care of my kids. That means a lot."

He stopped speaking and Linnie got on the phone. "Thanks again, Hailey. See you soon. This is the best Christmas that's ever happened to me. Love that the kids are happy with you."

"I'll have them ready for whenever you arrive."

"We should be there in a couple of hours. See you then."

After the call ended, Hailey sank onto the edge of the bed. The first time she'd met Linnie, they'd shared an instant connection. Funny, how things work out. Nick had been worried about the responsibility of having the kids here, but Hailey knew she'd done the right thing. She'd brought a family together.

When she entered the kitchen, Brady ran over to her. "Can we make a castle?"

She looked out at the rain and shook her head. "Not today. But we can draw some castles. Would you like that?"

Brady nodded with enthusiasm.

Hailey saw that Luna was settled and spoke to Nick about their plan before grabbing her phone and a cup of coffee. "Okay, Brady, let's go."

Hailey loved her studio. A separate space away from the house, it allowed her to leave paintings to dry away from prying eyes and fingers. Aside from the area where she painted, she had a desk that held her computer and other items that made her small office functional.

Hailey got Brady settled at a small table with a paper and crayon. "You can draw a castle while I do some office work. Here's a picture of a big sandcastle. See if you can draw one like it."

Brady grinned at her. "I think I can."

"Great." Hailey was curious to see what kind of talent he had. By the size and shape of him, she'd bet he'd inherited some of his father's athletic skills. But he'd also displayed a sense of appreciation for the shapes they used to make a castle, making her believe he might be artistic too.

Hailey went about checking emails, going over bills and expenses, and was busy making notes on the last picture she wanted to include in the book when she realized the time.

Trying not to seem alarmed, Hailey phoned Linnie. *No answer.*

"Are you ready for some lunch?" she asked Brady brightly.

He nodded and held up his picture to show her.

"Excellent." Hailey studied it. Brady had drawn something that slightly resembled a castle and what looked like a dog nearby. Still, Hailey could see enough detail to be impressed.

They raced through the rain to the house and into the kitchen.

Nick was holding Luna. "I was going to call you. Luna needs a diaper changed."

"Will you make Brady lunch while I take care of her?" Hailey asked. "And then we need to talk." She couldn't hide her worry.

Catching on, Nick said, "Okay. Just so you know, I-75 has been closed down due to an accident. I saw it on the news in my office. I don't have any details, but they said traffic is a nightmare."

"I tried to call her, but no answer."

Nick placed a hand on her shoulder. "I'm sure things are very chaotic there at the moment."

Luna fussed and cried, drawing Hailey's attention. She left the kitchen with her, telling herself that Nick was right. She wouldn't panic yet.

But later, after Luna had been changed, fed, and put down for a nap, and Brady was watching a television show after eating lunch, worry gnawed at Hailey's insides, making them raw. By now, Linnie or Mac should've called to explain. The only news about the accident was that it involved a tractor trailer truck and a car.

Hailey noticed Nick's worry, and nausea burned a path through her.

"What can we do?" she asked Nick quietly to keep from disturbing Brady.

He shrugged. "Do you have any idea what kind of car Linnie and Mac were riding in?"

"No," Hailey replied. "Linnie drives a Honda, but I don't know what kind of car Mac has."

"Well, let me call the state troopers and see if they can give us any information. Normally, detailed information is withheld until the next of kin is notified."

"But they don't have next of kin," Hailey said. "Please go ahead and call the state police. I can't stand waiting to hear." She didn't mention it, but a feeling of dread had infiltrated her body like a cold, wet fog, chilling every part of her.

"Hailey?"

She whipped around. Brady was standing in the doorway looking worried. "When is Mommy coming?"

"I don't know," Hailey said. "In the meantime, how about a chocolate chip cookie? I made some for the people at the library. But they won't miss one or two."

He didn't quite return her smile.

She led him into the kitchen, praying Nick could find answers—answers they liked.

When he joined them in the kitchen, Nick shook his head. "Nothing."

Hailey pressed her lips together, wanting to cry.

Though the tension in the air almost crippled her, Hailey somehow managed to get through the rest of the day. The evening news said the car in the accident was a sports car, though one couldn't tell from the way the car was crushed. Hailey's worries hitched up another notch. Wouldn't a football player like Mac have that kind of car?

Though Brady fought the idea, Hailey finally got him into a bath before helping him into pajamas. "Another sleepover," she said. "Zeke is really happy about that."

Brady lowered his head. When he lifted it, tears shone in his eyes. His lower lip trembled. "I thought Mommy was coming this morning."

"I did too," Hailey said honestly. "She's been delayed. We'll know more tomorrow."

Brady climbed under the lightweight blanket on his bed and clung to Charlie.

Zeke, bless his doggy heart, seemed to understand that Brady needed him, and when Hailey lifted him onto the bed, he snuggled up to Brady and kissed his cheek.

"I'll leave you for now. Nick and I will be in the living room. If you need me, call out and I'll come to you."

Brady yawned. "But Zeke can stay here. Right?"

"Right," Hailey replied. "He can be your sleep buddy."

When Hailey bent to kiss him, Brady wrapped his arms around her. She gave him an extra squeeze. "Sleep tight. Don't let the bed bugs …"

"Bite," finished Brady, smiling for the first time in a while.

Hailey tickled him, hoping to keep his spirits up.

He laughed and grew still. "Will Mommy wake me up when she comes?"

"We'll see," Hailey said, wondering if that would ever happen.

She and Nick were sitting in front of the television watching the videos of the accident scene when they heard a car pull into the driveway.

Heart pounding, Hailey raced to the door, flung it open, and stared at the car. Her knees buckled, and she felt herself falling.

Strong arms grabbed hold of her. "Steady," said Nick. "Let's hear what the State Trooper has to say."

She moved forward feeling as if she was in a nightmare. But the uniform of the man walking toward them with a grim expression was all too real.

"Can we go inside to talk?" the man asked, a gentleness to his voice that belied his physical size.

"Sure. Is this is relating to Linnie and Mac MacGrath?

"I'm afraid so," the trooper said. "We found a document inside Ms. MacGrath's purse that referred to you. She'd written your address along the edge of it."

"Better come in," said Nick. "But we need to be quiet. Both the kids are asleep."

Hailey hadn't known she was crying until she felt a wetness on her chin. She swiped at her eyes, but her vision remained blurry.

"It's going to be all right," Nick said, still keeping a firm hold on her.

But Hailey knew he was wrong.

CHAPTER 9

Hailey collapsed on the couch. "What are we going to do?" she asked, choking on her words. The trooper had left with a promise not to report the situation to the Department of Children and Families until they'd had time to digest their options. The thought of Brady and Luna being placed in foster care made her woozy.

"First, I think we should call Mike for advice about how to tell Brady. Mike's noted for his counseling work with children. He may know of a lawyer in Florida to handle a case like this."

Hailey sat up. "Okay, but, Nick, there's no way I'm letting someone else take these children away. We're perfectly capable of taking care of them."

"One thing at a time, Hailey. Don't worry. I'm on your side." Nick picked up his cell and made the call.

Her mind still reeling, Hailey heard Nick give the details to Mike. Unable to stop herself, she tiptoed to where Luna lay in her bed. Watching her breathe in and out, she knew she'd fight to keep her.

Next, she opened the door to Brady's room and peeked inside. He was sprawled across the bed holding onto Charlie.

Fresh tears sprang to her eyes. Poor little boy. She'd help him the best she could, but she knew it wouldn't be easy. They had a connection from the beginning, but losing his mother was something a child never got over.

When she went back to the living room, Nick was standing by the window staring out at the darkness. She went over to him and wrapped her arms around him. "What did Mike say?"

He looked down at her, his eyes swimming with tears. "We have to be honest without too many details. At his age, Brady doesn't need to know more than there's been an accident and ..." his voice hitched ... "and his mother is dead. We can help him remember good things about her, but he must know she's never coming back. It would be cruel to give him false hope." Nick ran a hand through his dark curls. "Mike also feels there shouldn't be a problem with our adopting them. With both Linnie and Mac being foster kids and with the signed document we have, their intent is clear. God! What a horrible thing this is for those kids."

"You're okay with taking Brady and Luna into our family? Making them ours?" Hailey held her breath. She knew Nick very well but needed to hear his words.

"Yes. I would never turn them away." He squeezed her. "Didn't think it would happen this way, but we've been given not one, but two kids to raise and love. I want to do this transition as seamlessly as possible for Brady."

"Thank you," said Hailey smiling at him.

"For what?"

"For being you." Hailey hugged him as tightly as she could. He was her rock.

Nick let out a long sigh. "We'd better try to get as much sleep as possible. Tomorrow is going to be a long day."

"Oh, no! Tomorrow is Christmas. What a way to spend our first Christmas with the kids." Hailey covered her face in her hands and released fresh tears.

Nick rubbed her shaking shoulders. "We can do this, Hailey. Together, like always."

Hailey lifted her face and studied him. She'd been right about him all along.

❄

Hailey somehow made it through the rest of the night without breaking down. Luna, bless her heart, woke up at four, had her bottle and a new diaper and went back to sleep until seven when Brady awoke.

He stumbled into the kitchen on bare feet, holding onto Charlie. "Where's Mommy?"

"I'll get Luna," offered Nick.

"Brady, we need to talk," said Hailey. She patted her legs.

He padded over to her. He hesitated for a moment and climbed into her lap.

Hailey wrapped her arms around him, sent a quick prayer for help, and held him close.

"Brady, your Mommy has been in an accident."

"Is she okay?" Brady asked, looking up at her with trusting eyes.

Hailey shook her head. "No. She was badly hurt and died. She's in heaven now."

Brady frowned. "But I want her here!"

"Me, too," said Hailey. "Do you remember the story about Charlie and his pet parakeet and how after the bird died, Charlie kept him in his thoughts?"

Brady's eyes widened as understanding grew. He pounded on her chest with his fists. "No! No! I want my Mommy now!"

Holding Luna, Nick came into the room and silently watched her struggle for the right words.

"It's okay to be upset, Brady, but it won't change this," said Hailey. "I'd give anything to make things different, but I

can't. I promise you and Luna will be safe with Nick and me."

Brady's gaze swung to Luna. "I said I'd take care of my baby sister."

"We're all going to take care of her. Both of you. I'm so, so, sorry, Brady."

She drew him up against her chest and rubbed his back. As he began to sob—sobs that broke her heart—Hailey rocked him back and forth in her arms and watched as Nick lifted the bottle she'd prepared for Luna and started feeding her.

She'd always wished for a family, but she never wanted it to happen like this.

When he stopped crying, Brady looked up at her and touched her wet cheek. Then he got off her lap and picked up his stuffed dog, hugging Charlie tightly. Gently, she wiped the tears from his face. "You'll be safe with us."

Later, Brady remained quiet as he lay on the couch in the living room staring at the television. Nick had talked to Brady separately, assuring him of their support and care, and then Brady didn't want to talk anymore.

To avoid speaking to them, Hailey texted a message to her mother and sisters, sending Christmas wishes along with a note that she'd be in touch with them later in the week. She didn't want to worry them, but she knew she couldn't talk about the situation without breaking down and sobbing. Right now, she couldn't allow herself that luxury.

She was about to call Janna when her name popped up on her caller ID screen.

"Hailey, I spoke to Mike, and he told me what's happened. How can I help?"

"Thanks, Janna. I would still like you and Mike and Zoey to come for dinner. I think it would be helpful to all of us."

"Okay. If you think of anything I can do before then, let me know."

"We'll have to move Luna's crib and baby equipment from

Linnie's rental to here. And I want to pack up Brady's things. I can use your help then. Maybe Mike could help with the furniture."

"Done deal," said Janna. "How's Brady? Such a darling little boy."

"He understands as much as he can, but he's in pain. Both Nick and I have spoken with him, assured him we're there for him, but he needs time to truly understand. Mike has been amazing about giving us advice."

"Mike is such a great guy," said Janna. "I'm glad he could help."

"See you later," said Hailey. "Gotta go. Luna's crying."

Hailey hung up thinking of Maddie. Her adopted mother had taken her in when she was eight-years-old. By then, she'd known a lot of broken promises. She vowed not to do the same to Brady.

After Hailey had taken a shower in which she'd allowed her tears to meld with the hot water, she decided the best thing to do was to keep Brady active.

She glanced through the window at the bright sunshine and knew what to do. Christmas dinner was under control. It was time to play a little with Brady.

Hailey went to Brady in the living room, sat on the edge of the couch beside him, and stroked his head.

"It's nice outside. Let's go make a sandcastle. What do you say? We'll make it a special one for your mother."

Brady studied her. "She's not coming back?"

"No," said Hailey, her heart breaking. "But we can do things to remember her. A castle in her honor might be very nice." She hoped she was saying the right things to him. She hadn't had any real experience with children and death except in her book about Charlie and his bird.

Brady reached out and touched her hand.

Hailey clasped his fingers, lifted his hand, and kissed it. "It's a very sad time, but Nick and I are going to take care of you and Luna."

"Promise?" Brady's eyes filled with tears and overflowed.

"Yes." Hailey's throat tightened. "I promise." She pulled him to her and held him, letting him cry.

"Shall I get the castle building equipment out?" she asked after several minutes had passed.

He looked up at her and nodded.

She got out a tissue and wiped the tears from his face before helping him to his feet. "Follow me."

While Brady looked through the canvas bag of beach tools, Nick came to her and spoke quietly. "I just got off the phone with Mike. He thinks it's a wise idea to bring Brady's things to our house to help him understand it's a permanent thing. While you and Janna stay with the kids, he and I'll gather the baby stuff, pack up Brady's things, and bring it here. They'll arrive in an hour or so."

Hailey closed her eyes to ease the stinging in them. "Okay. For the moment, we'll put Luna in one of the two free guest rooms."

Hailey turned to reach for her canvas bag and found Brady staring at her. "We'll bring your things and Luna's here, so you're comfortable," she explained.

Brady didn't say anything. He just turned and walked away.

Hailey let him go, understanding his need to be alone.

They met up at the sliding door leading to the lanai and beyond it to the beach. Zeke, who hadn't left Brady's side, went with them onto the sand.

It was an unseasonably warm day. People were walking on the beach. Some children appeared to be playing with new toys. Kites were dancing in the breeze, drawing Brady's attention. Hailey wondered how best to celebrate Christmas with him. Perhaps they'd celebrate on New Year's Day, so Brady's memory of this Christmas wouldn't forever ruin the holiday for him.

"This looks like the perfect spot for us to begin," said Hailey setting down the bag. "Do you remember what we did last time?"

Brady nodded and remained quiet.

She handed him a shovel and pail and took one of each for herself.

They filled the buckets. With a third bucket of water, they wet the sand in the buckets and dumped it. After repeating the process several times, they formed a mound of shapes that they could mold into a building and towers. Hailey showed Brady how to make windows and add detail to the towers.

When they were ready, she handed him a couple of flags she withdrew from the bag. "Here. You place them where you want."

Brady placed all three flags close together in the middle at the highest point.

"Great job," Hailey said. "Now, shall we place people inside?"

He studied her with a frown.

"I sometimes pretend people live there." With her finger, she drew a little boy in the wet sand.

"I want Mommy and me inside."

"All right. But I think we'd better place other people there too. How about Luna?"

Brady nodded. "Okay."

"And let's put Zeke, Nick, and me inside too so we can all be together like now. Even though Mommy isn't here in person, we'll keep her with us in our thoughts."

Brady looked in the distance and sighed. Tears streaked down his cheeks. "Can we go back now?"

"Sure. Help me rinse out the buckets, and we'll be ready

to go."

Back at the house, Luna was just waking up. "Glad you're here. Luna needs you," said Nick, handing her the smelly baby.

"Aw, little one. Let's get you cleaned up."

"I've put her things in the new bathroom she'll be using," said Nick.

"Thanks. Her bottle is ready. Can you heat it up for me? Be sure to test it," said Hailey, realizing she'd have to make more formula and clean more bottles.

When she went to change Luna, Hailey began a list of other things she'd need. Nick would bring the diaper pail from Linnie's house, but they were low on the diapers. In the past, she'd researched the basics that every baby needs, but she hadn't understood how fast babies went through diapers and clothes.

Hailey had just finished burping Luna and was getting ready to put her down for a nap when Janna arrived with a casserole and a large cloth bag stuffed with things for the meal.

"Mike and Zoey will be along. He's helping Nick load things up from the house. He said you'd go there later to make sure things are in order."

"That's the plan. It's such a horrendous occasion that I'm not looking forward to it. But I know I have to do it. I'm not sure when the lease on the house ends. Regardless, I want everything cleared out before the end of the month and the new year begins."

"May I see her?" Janna said, holding out her arms.

She handed the baby to Janna and peered down at her. "Isn't she beautiful?" In just a matter of days, Luna was filling out and looking less like a newborn.

"Oh, yes, she's lovely. How's her big brother doing?"

"He's in the living room watching television. It's hard to be sure, but I think he's taking in the information. He's very quiet. There have been tears from all of us, of course. I'm thankful Mike is willing to help him and us deal with this tragedy."

"It's such a horrible thing to happen to a child. To all of you, really."

Hailey's eyes filled. "I've always wanted a family, but this? I'm struggling too. Linnie and I were becoming good friends. When I last talked to her, she was ecstatic about getting back together with Mac. They were coming here to get the kids before moving to Miami to live."

"Life is so uncertain," sighed Janna. She gave the baby back to Hailey. "I want you to know I'm here for you."

"Thanks. That means a lot to me, especially with my family far away."

"Do your mom and your sisters know about this?"

"Not yet," said Hailey. "I have to keep myself together for Brady. I know if I talked to any of them, I'd break down completely."

"Understood. You're lucky. I wish I had a large family like yours."

"Oh, Janna, I want you to know that I consider you part of my family," said Hailey, her sincerity real. "How are you and Mike doing?"

"We're totally committed to continuing to see where our relationship can go. Can you believe it? After years of one disappointment after another, I've found a man who is everything I've ever wanted in a healthy relationship."

"That makes me very happy," said Hailey. "I'll be glad to see him. Zoey might help Brady. She's very outgoing, and he needs a friend right now."

"Fingers crossed it helps," Hailey said, wanting so much to take away any pain from Brady.

CHAPTER 10

W hen Hailey saw Zoey and Brady together, she knew Mike was right. Being with Zoey was exactly what Brady needed. They smiled at one another and began chatting as Nick and Mike passed them loaded down with items from the house. Thankfully, at the last minute, Linnie had taken Brady's car seat out of her car and given it to them. Luna's was in use inside.

"My daddy says you're sad. I don't have a mommy either," said Zoey. She glanced at Janna. "Maybe Janna."

Janna's face flushed.

Brady didn't say anything, but he took hold of Zoey's hand. "Want to play a game with me?"

They left the front entrance where they'd been standing and went down the hall to Brady's room. The ever-faithful Zeke followed at Brady's heels.

"Zoey's such a pleasant child," said Janna. "I'd love to become her mother."

"I have a feeling you will," said Hailey. "Why don't we go to the kitchen? I have some formula to prepare, and, frankly, I'd like a glass of wine."

"Sounds delicious to me. I can't imagine how stressed you

are. Are you leaving the gifts under the Christmas tree until later?"

"Yes. I'm not sure how we're going to handle Christmas."

"It's all heart-rending. By next year, things will be entirely different."

"I can't think that far ahead," said Hailey. "I'm going to take things one day at a time."

"Smart idea," said Janna. "I brought both red and white wine. Which do you prefer?"

"Let's save the white wine for the turkey and have some red wine now. I've set out some glasses."

While Hailey mixed up formula and poured it into enough newly-washed bottles to last through the night, Janna opened the pinot noir and poured them each a glass.

Together she and Janna worked out a plan for the meal and set the large dining room table. As they worked, Hailey thought once more about Janna being like a sister to her. Gratitude filled her. It had seemed very strange not to be in Granite Ridge with her family for the holidays. Now, it all made sense in a "meant-to-be" way.

Nick and Mike entered the kitchen.

"Zoey and Brady are playing nicely together," said Nick. "It's great to see."

"Did you get all the baby equipment set up?" Hailey asked.

"Yes," Nick answered. "Mike's already forewarned me that all this stuff is just the beginning."

"You and I are going to be busy shopping for the next couple of days. Tomorrow, after I check the house, I'll have a better idea of what exactly we need," said Hailey.

"Beer?" Nick asked Mike.

Mike nodded at him and turned his attention to her. "How are you doing, Hailey? It's a pretty emotional time."

Fresh tears stung her eyes. "It's all so sudden, and I have to admit I'm exhausted. But I'll do anything to make the transition as easy as possible for Brady. Luna's too young to realize what's happening, but Brady will need some help." She told them about building the castle and placing people inside it. "I hope I did the right thing."

"Sounds that way. I'll try to follow up with Brady on that idea and let you know," Mike said.

"Thank you," said Hailey. "It was a lucky day when Janna met you, and we all became friends."

Mike's cheeks grew pink, and Hailey realized he wasn't used to being on the receiving end of such compliments. It made her like him even more.

❄️

After a dinner filled with talk that took her mind away from her worries, watching Brady and Zoey interact, and knowing she had friends behind her, Hailey stood in the kitchen with Janna cleaning up.

"That was delicious," said Janna.

"I'm thankful Nick is comfortable in the kitchen. I couldn't do it without his help." Hailey cast a glance at Nick in the living room. He was sitting on the couch feeding Luna and chatting with Mike. "And it's great that he's used to infants after helping his sister with Regan."

"It will be nice for Brady to have cousins," said Janna.

Hailey's breath caught. She hadn't answered any calls from her family. Even though she'd sent a message saying she'd talk to them tomorrow, it didn't seem right. Maybe later, after Brady was in bed and Luna was settled, she'd be able to do it.

After they loaded the dishwasher and pans were left to soak, Hailey turned to Janna. "How about a cup of tea?"

"That sounds perfect," said Janna. "And then we'll have to go. Zoey is about to fall asleep."

Hailey hugged her. "I'm very grateful for everything you

and Mike have done for us." She stood back and shook her head. "I still can't believe all that's happened. Thanks for suggesting Owen Sheehan as our family law lawyer. I'm going to talk to my sister, Jo, about the situation, but it's wise to have someone familiar with Florida law to help us."

"I've known Owen and his father for years. He's the best in the business," said Janna.

Hailey let out a long sigh. "It's such a tragedy. Linnie was very excited about the future."

"I'm happy she knew her children were being well taken care of," said Janna. "I can't imagine a mother in her situation not knowing that."

Hailey glanced at Brady coloring with Zoey. Her eyes filled as they had many times during the day. She'd be the best mother she could to both Brady and his baby sister.

That night, after Brady was asleep and she'd fed Luna. Hailey sat alone in the kitchen. It was ten o'clock in Florida; eight o'clock in Granite Ridge. She decided not to call Jo. Her questions and traumatic story could wait. No point in ruining Christmas for her.

Hailey stared into the dark. Stars were twinkling in the sky, sending silent messages from heaven. "I promise to take care of your children, Linnie," she whispered, thinking how short life was, how it was meant to be fully experienced. She was luckier than most. She had an awesome husband, an exciting career, and was financially stable. All sound reasons to help others.

Her cell rang. *Alissa.*

Hearing her voice, Hailey cried softly. "Oh, Alissa. I need you. You've always been a comfort to me. When we were kids, you let me climb into bed with you." Her voice hitched. "You even shared your unicorn pillow. Remember?"

"I do, but, Hailey, what's wrong?"

Hailey told her the entire story. When she was through, there was silence on the other end of the call.

"Alissa?"

"Hold on," said Alissa. "I need a tissue." When she came back on the call, Alissa said, "That's unbelievable, simply awful. What can I do to help you?"

"Just listen to me from time to time. You're such a good mom. I've promised to try my best. As I told you earlier, Brady and I have a connection already, but I can't take the place of his mother."

"You will in time," said Alissa. "But we don't want him to forget the woman she was. Is his father really a famous football player?"

"Yes. He's Mac MacGrath, which presents its own set of problems. But he acknowledged both Brady and Luna were his. They were all going to live together."

"Have you talked to Mom or Jo?" Alissa asked.

"Not yet. I didn't want to spoil Christmas for them or any of you." Hailey sniffled. "How about your Christmas? Is it going well with Jed's parents?"

"We did our best, but they attacked both of us and had the nerve to tell Jed they want to merge his business into the family business. We ended up leaving and are staying at a hotel in downtown Seattle. Anyway, I'll tell you all the details later. You have enough on your plate."

"Love you, sis. I've got to go. The baby is crying," said Hailey, surprised all over again by her situation. She'd imagined such a different scenario when she had a baby in the house.

The after-Christmas call to her mother was difficult. She didn't want her to worry. But when Maddie offered to fly to Florida to help her, tears stung Hailey's eyes.

"That would be wonderful. But let's wait until after the new year. I want to get things more settled. I've set up doctor's appointments for them, and we need to speak to our lawyer. When the time comes, I'll meet you at the airport." Hailey paused to wipe her tears away. "Love you, Mom."

"Love you, too. I'll talk to you soon to let you know what arrangements I make. I'm anxious to meet the children, and I want to make sure you're all right. Call me anytime you want. I'm here for you."

"Okay. See you soon." Ending the call, Hailey was filled with gratitude for having someone like Maddie in her life. All she'd needed to hear was her mother's support, then Hailey knew everything would be all right. The Kirby women were strong.

Nick walked into the kitchen. "Brady and I will buy the baby equipment on the list we made. You're going to pick up things like clothing later. Right?"

Hailey nodded and handed him the list. "Yes. I'll do the rest after I get a chance to go to the house."

"Brady keeps talking about some of the toys left behind there," said Nick. "I think we need to bring those home."

"I'll pack up as much as I can. I'll probably have to clean the house a little each day. It helps that you have a holiday break at school. We're going to need to do this transition together."

"No problem. I've got a call in at Owen Sheehan's office."

"I've started a list of items we need to discuss with him. Considering the signed document and the fact that both Linnie and Mac were products of the foster care system, it shouldn't be too difficult to proceed with adoption plans. Owen should be able to help with those details."

"A lot to think about," said Nick, shaking his head.

"You're not considering anything else but adoption, are you?" asked Hailey, giving him a steady look. They'd barely had time to discuss it.

"No, of course not. It feels right." He kissed her. "See you later. I'll take Brady with me. And later, we'll have to do something about Christmas for him, maybe talk to him about waiting a few days. I'll see how it goes and try to get some ideas for him. All the after-holiday sales are going on."

Pleased by Nick's willingness to help, Hailey rose from her seat at the kitchen table to talk to Brady. He was playing with Zeke in the living room.

"Nick said you're going on errands with him. Have fun! You can help him pick out things for the baby."

Brady gave her a steady look. "I promised to take care of Luna."

"I know. We'll all do that together. I don't want you to worry about it. That job isn't yours alone. Nick and I will help, too."

The lines of worry eased from Brady's brow. He let out a sigh. "Okay."

"C'mon, buddy," said Nick. "Let's go. And if we do a quick job, there might be time for a treat for us."

"'Bye, Zeke," said Brady, rubbing his ears. "See you later."

Zeke barked and sat at Hailey's heels with a doleful look as Brady and Nick left. After they were gone, the dog trotted to the baby's room.

Hailey watched him, touched by his devotion to the kids.

CHAPTER 11

Hailey unlocked the door to Linnie's rental and walked inside feeling as if she should tiptoe. It felt strange being in the house when Linnie would never be there again. It would feel even worse to go through the kids' rooms and pack their things. She'd brought a box and a couple of large garbage bags with her.

Luna's room was mostly empty after having the crib, changing table, and diaper pail moved to her house. Only one bureau remained. Hailey opened the top drawer and swallowed a gasp at its emptiness. Looking through the three remaining drawers, she found very few items. And when she checked the closet, only two dresses on hangers caught her attention.

Hailey shook her head with dismay. She knew Linnie had been struggling with her situation, but she hadn't realized how unprepared she was for the baby. If Linnie had lived, her life would have been very different—both financially and emotionally secure. These circumstances were such a tragedy in many ways.

She packed Luna's things in a bag and moved to Brady's room where she carefully placed the last of his clothing and the rest of his toys, books, and games into the bag. She planned to save anything of value, like jewelry, for the kids to have later in their lives. She thought of Mac and wondered what his agent might know about his private life. She'd have her lawyer get in touch with him.

Hailey held her breath as she entered Linnie's room. The unmade bed held a pillow with an indentation. "I'm sorry," Hailey whispered as she searched for any paperwork she could find. She knew documentation would be important to the case.

She found an expandable file in a lower drawer of the bureau. Hoping Linnie was meticulous about keeping records, Hailey lifted the file, set it on the bed, and opened it. Inside were several documents. She found a marriage license, birth certificates with Mac's name on them for both kids, even a copy of the lease. The rental included the furniture except for what Linnie had bought for Luna, and it was a month-to-month lease. Relief sent a sting to her eyes as she examined more papers. "Bless you," Hailey whispered before letting her tears flow, saddened to realize the file contained Linnie's entire life in just a handful of documents.

Pulling herself together, Hailey checked the closet in the room and found nothing out of the ordinary. She carried the file down the hall to where she'd left the bag of things she'd gathered. As she did, she noticed the closet in the hall, stopped, and opened it.

Inside, she spied brightly-wrapped Christmas packages. Hailey's vision blurred. It could've been the best Christmas ever for that family. Instead, it was a disaster.

Hailey tucked the gifts into the second bag she'd brought and carried them to the car as an idea circled in her mind.

After loading everything she'd packed into the car, Hailey locked up the house and headed to one of the big-box stores in the area. She needed to stock up on onesies, blankets, sheets, and the rest of the items on her list, including a couple of delightful girlie outfits for Luna. She'd order more online later.

On the way home, she called Nick. "Hi. How're things there? Is Luna okay?"

"I just fed and changed her. She's down for a nap," Nick responded, pride in his voice. "Brady is playing in his room."

"Great. I need you to get Brady out of the house while I carry my purchases and the Christmas gifts that I found in Linnie's rental inside. I need enough time to hide the presents under the Christmas tree. We'll open them this evening."

"Okay. He's been wondering about Santa Claus and Christmas and if he'll get anything this year."

"Then, this will be something fun for him. I should be home in about ten minutes. See you then."

Brady was too busy playing with the toys she'd brought from the house to notice the gifts she'd carefully placed beneath the Christmas tree. After discussing it with Nick, they decided to open them before dinner, telling Brady Santa Claus had dropped them off here.

"Do you think he'll be suspicious when we tell him Santa got the message to come here with his gifts?" said Nick. "He's a pretty sensible boy."

"I think it'll depend on how we play it," said Hailey. "Maddie put the magic into Christmas for me when I was eight years old, a time when some kids know the truth about Santa. Even as an adult, I still believe in Santa Claus because he's the spirit of giving. We all need that at any age."

Nick pulled her to him. "Ah, Hailey. I love you."

"Love you too. I don't know what I'd do if you didn't like kids or weren't great with them."

"Luna and Brady will always be our 'firstborns'," he said.

"And you will always be the love of my life," said Hailey, knowing no matter what happened in the time to come, she'd be by his side.

Later that afternoon, Hailey sat on the floor with Nick, Brady, and Luna near the Christmas tree in the living room. Zeke lay beside them drifting off to sleep, exhausted from his guarding duties.

"Santa left presents for me here?" asked Brady, his eyes shining with excitement.

"Yes," said Hailey, wrapping an arm around him. "He's magical. He must've known you were staying here now."

Brady drew a breath and studied her. "Can he bring Mommy back?"

Blinking rapidly, Hailey shook her head. "I'm sorry. No. That's the one thing he can't do. But I have a feeling she'd be happy for you. Shall we open some now?"

Brady nodded, but there was no smile. Hailey's heart ached for him.

Soon the eager boy inside Brady emerged, and he had a great time opening gifts for him and Luna. He watched as Nick handed Hailey a gift, and they shared a kiss.

When she saw the way Brady was studying them, Hailey turned to him. "Nick and I love each other. And we love you, too."

Brady gave her a sweet smile. "Okay."

Having kept words bottled inside herself as a young child, she knew what a big statement that was. "That makes me very happy." She cradled his face in her hands and kissed his cheek. She didn't want to rush Brady, didn't want to make him feel he couldn't grieve, but this connection was precious to her.

While Brady played with his new toys, Hailey gave Nick his gift and then couldn't help staring at the pendant he'd given her. It was a gold heart with a bar of three diamonds attached to it. "I thought it would represent you, me, and a baby. Now it'll represent Brady, Luna, and the baby we'll have one day."

"Oh, that's precious," Hailey murmured, not wanting to think about a baby of their own right now. She was exhausted physically and emotionally.

Nick loved the watch she'd given him. "I thought you could use it when you went running. Now, maybe it'll help you keep time with Brady and Luna's schedule."

They hugged one another. Their lives had been turned upside down.

The next day, Owen Sheehan returned Nick's call with an apology for not getting back to them sooner. They talked about the case, and Owen agreed to meet at the house later that morning. The one fear Hailey had was that the kids would somehow be turned over to the foster care system.

Later, sitting in the kitchen with them, Owen looked through all the documentation they gave him and assured them they needn't worry about the children being taken from them.

"I'll put together an adoption profile for you and appear before the judge. If he approves, we'll make an appointment for you to go before the court for final adoptions. We won't have to follow all the normal steps, but he'll need reassurance that all is in order and meets the needs of the children. Background checks and home inspections will be done, that sort of thing. Mind if I take a few pictures of the house—the kids' rooms in particular? Then I'll speak with Brady for a few minutes if that's all right with you. You may remain part of the conversation if you wish."

Nick looked at her. "That sounds okay. Right, hon?"

"Yes, but we need to talk about finances for the kids," Hailey said. "We, of course, will assume financial responsibility for them. But Mac was making a lot of money, which we'll protect for the kids. I have no idea what Mac's personal situation was, but his agent should know."

"You're right. This is important," agreed Owen. "A financial manager should be able to set up a trust for them. The woman who handles my account is a whiz at doing this, protecting money, and establishing something that makes sense. For instance, any monies for the kids could be used for their education. If you'd like, I can set up a meeting with her for you. Another thing, we don't want information to get out about where the kids are. Creeps love to take advantage of circumstances like this, even claiming to be relatives, thinking there's money in it for them."

"Oh my God! I don't want any spotlight on the children," said Hailey. "Brady has enough to deal with; he doesn't need any publicity. That would be cruel. He's normally quite shy."

Owen sighed and shook his head. "I'll do my best. I'll know more after I talk to Mac's agent and the people behind the football franchise."

Brady came running into the kitchen. "Nick! Come see what I made."

Nick grinned and got to his feet. "Are you talking about a spaceship?"

"Yep. It's a cool one."

"Santa brought Brady a jumbo-sized Lego set. Excellent for fingers his age," Hailey explained.

"Hi, Brady. I'm Mr. Sheehan," said Owen. "Can I come and see too?"

Brady hesitated and looked to Hailey.

"It's all right. He's a family friend," said Hailey.

"Okay," Brady said.

As they left the room, Luna's cries came through the baby monitor. Hailey went to her.

Luna was lying on her back, waving her little fists in the air as if she could use them to give orders.

"Such a little dictator," crooned Hailey. "But we love you, baby girl."

Luna stopped thrashing and stared at her.

Hailey's breath caught. Luna was beginning to recognize her.

Nick and Owen walked into the room as she finished diapering Luna. "Eventually, we'll decorate the kids' rooms. There hasn't been a chance to do that." Hailey knew she was babbling, but Owen's presence made her nervous. He'd see that the kids were comfortable with them, wouldn't he?

She lifted Luna to her shoulder and headed to the kitchen to warm the formula, feeling more at ease with Luna than she had just a few days ago. Had it been only that short time? It had seemed an endless circle of feeding, sleeping, and changing.

After Owen left, the bright sun sent welcoming rays inside the kitchen. Hailey closed her eyes and drew a deep breath. A walk along the beach was exactly what she needed.

She went to Brady's room where Nick and Brady were working together on another spaceship. "I'm going for a walk on the beach. Anyone want to come?"

Nick and Brady shook their heads.

"You go," said Nick. "We're doing a great job here."

Content to be alone, Hailey left and walked out to the sand. The salty tang of the air filled her lungs and loosened the tight muscles around her neck and shoulders. She headed down the beach at a stroll, savoring each meandering step, her mind full of thoughts about the days ahead.

She couldn't get caught up in the fear of losing the kids. Everyone agreed it seemed a clear-cut case. But she knew what the idea of fame and fortune could do to twisted minds. No matter who came forward to claim the kids, she would stay strong. Linnie had never mentioned other family or close friends during their conversations.

At the sound of Nick's voice, she turned.

"Here comes Zeke. He couldn't stand to be left behind." Nick let go of the leash attached to Zeke's harness and the little dog charged toward her like a black and tan bullet across the sand.

Laughing, Hailey bent down to greet him.

He reached her, and she swept him up in her arms. "Zeke, do you need a break too?"

He kissed her cheek and then wiggled to get down.

She set him on the sand, and they headed down the beach together.

Small shorebirds scooted on the sand ahead of them, moving quickly as they searched for food. The cries of the seagulls above her sounded mournful and then less so as her emotions calmed. A horrible tragedy had taken place, changing lives forever. There'd always be cause for sadness, but Hailey made a promise to herself that there would be joy too. Brady and his sister were bright, beautiful children who were unexpectedly hers. She'd make sure to be thankful for them after struggling for a baby of her own.

Hailey stopped and listened to the sound of the waves kissing the shore and pulling back. This time, it sounded like a lullaby.

CHAPTER 12

"Are you sure?" Janna asked Hailey.

"Absolutely. It will be a treat for Brady to have Zoey spend the night. They can celebrate New Year's Eve together. We'll have a little party here, which will give you and Mike a chance to have the entire evening without worrying about Zoey or a babysitter." Hailey chuckled. "Who knows? I might get a little more sleep."

"Are you still lying down with Brady to help him get to sleep?" asked Janna.

"Yes. Mike says Brady feels safe with us. He's very affectionate with both Nick and me."

"That's nice to hear. I'll talk to Mike about New Year's Eve. I can't make that decision for him."

"I just wanted your input. Now that I know you're up for it, I'll call Mike myself. Things are going very well between the two of you."

"It's been unbelievable. We've talked and talked about everything. I know it might seem sudden to everyone else, but I think Mike may propose. It's like we've been waiting for each other all along. I know it sounds like a romance novel, but it's true."

"Well, then, I love being part of it. And thanks. Having Zoey here will be a big treat for Brady. They play well together, and I think it gives him comfort to know that Zoey understands what he's going through."

Pleased with the idea, Hailey called Mike with her offer.

"Sounds good, great even," he said. "Thanks."

"We're happy to do it after all the help you've given us. Drop Zoey off sometime in the afternoon. You can pick her up on the first whenever it's convenient. We'll let the kids stay up late, and, hopefully, they'll sleep in."

"How are you doing with all the changes?" Mike asked in the soft, gentle voice that he used when talking to patients.

"I'm exhausted. Nick has been very helpful, but I worry about handling everything when he goes back to his normal schedule this week."

"You can hire help, can't you?" he said.

"Yes, but I don't want to do that until I feel Brady's secure enough to handle someone new."

"Start slowly," he advised. "If you need a list of names, I have a few graduate students who need the money and who I think would work well with Brady."

"Thanks," Hailey said, glad she had a friend like Mike. A man who was making Janna the happiest she'd been in years.

While Nick watched Luna, Hailey took Brady to a party store to pick out hats and noisemakers for their celebration. Brady looked wide-eyed at the brightly colored selection. Hailey remembered the first time she'd gone shopping with Maddie for Christmas gifts for her sisters. It had seemed magical.

They walked through the store picking up paper plates, napkins, silly hats, and noisemakers. It had been an easier day. Brady had already helped Hailey make a cake using a mix. He'd also helped himself to a swipe of icing and sprinkled some rainbow-colored candies on top of the white frosting.

Zoey arrived with a pink, rolling suitcase. Brady grabbed her hand, and they ran off to his room, leaving her suitcase behind.

Smiling at them, she turned to Mike. "This is going to be good for both of them."

"Zoey hasn't been to many sleepovers, so this is pretty big stuff for her," he said. "If you need to call me for any reason, please do."

"Planned anything special?" Hailey asked, unable to stop herself from prying.

He grinned, and his eyes twinkled. "We'll see. I hope so."

"Well, Happy New Year, to you and Janna."

"Thanks." He started to say something else and stopped.

Hailey simply smiled. If she was right about her suspicions, Janna might become engaged tonight. She hoped so.

After dinner, Nick and Hailey helped Zoey and Brady get into their pajamas and got them settled in front of the television. Special New Year shows were on all the channels.

Zoey wore a tiara over her dark-brown curls, and Brady sported a bat hat with wings. They looked ridiculously cute, Hailey thought, and went to get Luna for another feeding while Nick took pictures of them.

"We can stay up as late as we want, can't we?" said Brady.

Hailey chuckled as she left the room. She and Nick had bets as to how late the two kids would last before falling asleep. But it was fun for them to believe they'd be able to ring in the new year.

Later, after Brady and Zoey were in their beds, Hailey and Nick sat on the couch in the living room listening to quiet music. They'd decided not to go the noisy route, not after facing the challenges of the coming year.

"I love you," said Nick, checking his watch. "Do you mind if we just go to bed now?"

"Not at all. I couldn't wait for you to ask. I just want to sleep." She looked at the disappointment on Nick's face and laughed. "If you hurry, we can make it better than that."

He picked her up and carried her into the bedroom. "I'll take care of the lights and check on the kids later. I don't want to miss a minute of making love to you."

She reached up and caressed his cheek. Neither did she.

As she'd suspected, the new year became even more hectic.

On January 3rd, her mother called. "I'm ready to visit if you are ready to have me."

"Oh, Mom, I'll be ecstatic to see you. They're marvelous kids, but I'm so tired."

"It's just the beginning, but I know you can do it, Hailey. I'll text you my flight information."

"Fantastic! I'll meet you at Tampa International Airport. If I can't make it, Nick will be there."

New energy filled Hailey as she went about cleaning up from the holidays. She was in the middle of putting away the last of the Christmas tree ornaments when she received a call from Mike.

"Hi, how are you, Mr. Engaged Man?" she said.

He laughed. "Pretty darn happy. But the reason I'm calling is that Zoey asked if Brady could come to her pre-school with her. It seems she was talking to him about it, and he wants to go. If he feels ready, it might be wise. He's a bright boy. I could pick you both up and introduce you to the owners. As you can imagine, I vetted the place carefully."

"I'll talk to Brady and call you right back. If he wants to go, that would be terrific and a big help to me."

Hailey ended the call and went to talk to Brady. He was lying on the floor in the living room, playing with his Legos while watching a *Mr. Rogers Neighborhood* rerun.

"Hey, Brady, I have some exciting news. If you want to go to Zoey's pre-school, Zoey's dad will pick you and me up to go take a look at it."

Brady jumped to his feet. "Yes! I want to go."

"Okay, then. Get your shoes and socks. I'll quickly get dressed."

At the school, Mike introduced Hailey to the owners and staff. He'd already alerted them to the circumstances.

Hailey was impressed with the friendly, clean atmosphere and the kids' enthusiasm as they participated in various activities. Brady stayed at Zoey's side for a while and then participated in a project with two other boys.

When it was time to go, an aide called to him, "Brady, better come. Your mother is ready to go now."

Brady stopped, stared at the aide, then at Hailey.

Hailey waited to see what other reaction would follow. Brady came over to her without saying anything and followed her out of the building.

On the way home, Brady was quiet in the car.

After Mike dropped them off, Brady took her hand as they walked to the front door. "Are you my mother now?"

Hailey knelt in front of him and took him in her arms. "Is that all right with you?"

"Yes," he said, hugging her close. "Luna, too?"

"Of course," Hailey replied, her vision blurring. "And Nick is your daddy now."

Brady gave her a steady look. "I like him too."

"That makes me very happy, Brady," said Hailey, holding in her emotions as best she could.

"I know." With one finger Brady tenderly wiped a tear from her cheek.

"We couldn't ask for a better boy to call our own," Hailey said, giving him another squeeze before getting to her feet.

Later, when Hailey told Nick what had happened, they both had tears in their eyes.

As Hailey watched her mother cross the floor to her at the airport, she felt like a child again waiting to be rescued.

"I'm glad you're here," said Hailey, hugging her hard.

"I'm happy to be here." Maddie studied her. "You look exhausted. I'm here to give you some rest and to see those adorable children."

"Oh, Mom, they're so beautiful!"

"It's cute of you to send so many pictures. C'mon. Let's go see them."

As Hailey had suspected all along, Maddie fell in love with Brady and Luna. It was touching to see Brady interact with her. A retired high school counselor, Maddie seemed to know exactly what to say and do to make Brady comfortable with her and his new situation. Watching them together, Hailey's eyes stung with tears remembering how Maddie had helped an eight-year-old bespectacled girl learn to open up her heart and mind to a new life.

As the days passed, Brady and Hailey showed Maddie how to make a sandcastle. After they finished and Brady put the flags on top, Hailey said, "Now, we place people inside." She turned to Brady. "Who goes in first? You and Zeke?"

He grinned. "And Zoey. And Mommy and Daddy and Luna." He eyed Maddie through his thick eyelashes and smiled shyly. "And Grandma, too." He paused.

Hailey wondered if he was thinking of Linnie, but the moment passed when Zeke threw himself into Brady's lap, knocking him back in his enthusiasm.

As Brady and Zeke chased each other on the beach, Maddie turned to Hailey. "What a lovely way to show Brady that he's part of a family. I'll have to remember that."

"I just want him to be happy, you know?" Hailey's lips trembled.

Maddie threw an arm across Hailey's shoulder. "You're doing a beautiful job of helping him deal with a horrible loss. I can see how much Brady loves you."

"It's funny," said Hailey. "We connected right from the beginning, almost as if fate had played a part."

"Fate or not, enjoy the children. I remember going through the same trial period with all of you girls. Look how that turned out."

"Because of you, Mom."

"The same thing will happen because of you, Hailey."

Sorry her mother's visit would be short, Hailey wrapped her arm around her mother, and they walked back to the house arm in arm.

A week later, as a surprise, Nick flew his sister, Stacy, and his six-year-old niece, Regan, to Florida for a few days of winter break. Hailey was thrilled to see them and loved how tender Regan was with Brady and how she loved holding the baby and feeding her. With the free moments it gave her, Hailey decided to call Mike for babysitting suggestions. The deadline for her book was coming up, and she needed the help.

For the rest of the winter weeks, Hailey kept in touch with

her sisters, especially Alissa, who'd had a disappointing holiday visit with Jed's parents.

One day, Alissa called her and announced she and Jed were taking a trip to Paris to celebrate Valentine's Day.

"That's great," Hailey said, totally thrilled for her. "And after that, during the first week of April, you'll be here for our girls' weekend. I can't wait!

"Me either," said Alissa. "I can't believe you have a child older than mine. They're both adorable and all yours now. Right?"

"Pretty much," Hailey said proudly. "The adoption is moving along smoothly. Thank goodness, the judge doesn't want to keep us waiting and waiting."

They chatted for a while longer, and when the call ended, Hailey let out a little sigh. Alissa and Jed were a great couple. A trip to Paris sounded so-o-o romantic.

Hailey thought about her own life. Long, romantic strolls, sipping glasses of wine lying naked in front of the fireplace, and spontaneous lovemaking were all things of the past. She'd tried a few times to stage something romantic, but either the baby cried, or Brady needed something, or one or both of them were too tired. But no matter how rushed, they found time to show one another their love in both little ways and big.

CHAPTER 13

Things were going well. Brady loved school, and Hailey's new babysitter, Taylor Ryder, took care of Luna four mornings a week so Hailey could work. Though her editor was touched by the story of Hailey's new life, she wasn't about to let Hailey off the hook on the deadline they'd agreed on for the seashore book.

On the day the manuscript was due, Hailey emailed the text and overnighted the paintings to her editor. Hailey thought it might be some of her best work because the scenery had taken on a new dimension after seeing it through Brady's eyes.

One afternoon, Brady came home with a cold and sore throat.

"Not to worry," said one of the teachers when she called the next day. "It's one of the hazards of pre-school."

But each day that passed with Brady staying home brought more and more tension into the house.

"I don't care! I want to go to school," screamed Brady when she told him he had to stay home one more day.

"I'm sorry, Brady, but we can't give this nasty cold to the other kids," Hailey said.

"No! I don't wanna live here anymore!" Brady cried, running into his room and slamming the door.

Hailey rocked back on her heels, stunned and hurt by his remark. *Was this about school or something deeper?* They'd all been surprised by the way that Brady had accepted his new life but had attributed it to Hailey and Brady being friends before the accident.

Hailey tapped on Brady's door. "May I come in?"

Hearing no answer, she opened it slowly and stopped.

Brady was lying on the bed, hugging his stuffed dog, crying.

Hailey entered the room and sat down on the edge of the bed. Gently, she rubbed his back. "I know things have been hard, very different for you over these past few months. I'm sorry. I wish you hadn't had to go through these changes."

He rolled over and looked up at her, worry creasing his broad brow. "Are you mad at me? Are you going away too?"

"Aw, sweetheart, no. Your mother didn't want to leave you, and I promise Nick and I are happy that you and Luna are part of our lives. That doesn't mean you can always have your way. Things don't work like that. When you're better, you can go to school. In the meantime, there are activities you can do at home. Taylor has already come up with a few ideas for you."

Brady let out one of the saddest sighs Hailey had ever heard.

She pulled him onto her lap. "I love you, Brady, and I'm very proud of all you're doing to help me out."

He looked up at her. "To the moon and back?"

"Oh, yes, and beyond to where your spaceships fly, and even beyond that."

She hugged him, and they cried together.

As the days drew closer to April, Hailey grew more and more excited. She loved all her sisters, but Alissa was special to her. As the youngest in the Kirby household, they'd quickly bonded. They'd slept in the same room and were more in sync with one another's activities.

One night, as Hailey sat at the kitchen table making a list of all the things she wanted to do during Alissa's visit, she turned to Nick. "I want to show Alissa a special quiet time, but we'll have to make do with staying in my studio as much as we can for any privacy. Taylor has agreed to be available day and night for the period Alissa is here, but it won't be the same."

Nick's eyes gleamed as he smiled. "I have a better plan. A friend of mine told me about a place for rent not too far from here. It's called the Seashell Cottage. It's very nice. I checked and was able to reserve several weeknights there. Are you interested?"

Hailey jumped up from her seat at the table and threw herself into his arms. "Interested? It sounds perfect. Thank you! Thank you!"

"Wow! I should've done something like this sooner," quipped Nick. "You haven't thrown yourself at me like this since ..."

"Since the kids came here," Hailey finished for him. "But Valentine's Day was unbelievable with Mike and Janna babysitting the kids, giving us the first free night we'd had in ages."

A slow, sexy grin crossed Nick's face. "Yeah, that was really great."

Hailey laughed. They'd had a fantastic time together.

The night before she was to fly to Florida, Alissa called. "I can't wait to see you and Nick, meet the kids, and have some private time. I really need a break. I love my kids, but I haven't been the same since we got back from Paris. It's the jet lag thing, plus moving our clocks ahead a couple of weeks ago. I can't seem to be on my usual schedule. The kids are going crazy being housebound inside with the latest storms. It's been a long winter."

"I was going to wait and surprise you, but Nick has rented us a house nearby right on the beach and with a swimming pool. And it's not too far from the Salty Key Inn where excellent food is the norm any time of day."

"Ohhh, now you're talking. That sounds fabulous. I'll try and sleep on the plane. See you tomorrow. Hugs to everyone, especially that husband of yours for coming up with something like this,"

Hailey laughed. Nick had always thought Alissa, like the others, was a great sister to Hailey.

The next afternoon, as planned, Hailey stood in the baggage claim area, waiting for Alissa to appear. She felt like a young girl awaiting her first big birthday party. It was sometimes difficult living away from family, and this was an exciting day for her.

When Hailey saw her sister walking toward her inside the Tampa airport, she ran toward her, arms outstretched. She and Alissa shared a special bond. Seeing her now, memories filled Hailey's mind—sweet memories of two young girls supporting one another during difficult times. With her shoulder-length dark hair, sparkling brown eyes, and petite figure, Alissa was as beautiful now as she'd always been.

They swayed back and forth in a hug, laughing and crying at the same time.

"It's been forever since we've been together," said Hailey,

though in truth it had been little more than a year. "I can't wait for you to meet Brady and Luna. They're so adorable."

Alissa smiled. "I can't wait to see them. Hailey, it's wonderful you have a family at last. You've always wanted one of your own."

"Heaven knows I didn't think it would happen this way, but I'm glad Nick and I are able to help them. It seems right, you know? And we love them so much."

"You're the perfect couple to do this. Nick has always been great with kids."

"Kids and dogs," Hailey said happily.

When they pulled apart, Alissa's eyes were shiny with tears. Hailey blinked away her own and took hold of her sister's free arm. "C'mon! Girls' weekend is about to begin."

"I took you at your word and only packed a few beachy things and one nice dress."

"Great. We can do a lot of different things at Seashell Cottage, but first, after we get there, let's walk the beach and catch up."

"Okay, and then we'll take naps."

Hailey laughed. "Are you as tired as I am? I don't know how you do it, Alissa. Two babies very close together. At least Brady is old enough to be able to do some things for himself."

"Well, I certainly don't plan on having more kids right away." She gave Hailey a teasing smile. "Maybe not until the two I have can take care of a new, little one."

Hailey shook a playful finger at her. "I know you too well, Alissa. You're a great mom. You'd never turn a baby over to anyone else."

"Never to my mother-in-law," said Alissa as they waited for luggage to arrive on the rotating baggage belt.

Hailey listened as Alissa described more of her visit to Jed's parents over the holiday.

"Poor you. Are you ever going to be able to reconcile with them?"

"I honestly don't know," Alissa said. "But enough of them. Let's enjoy ourselves. And I can't wait to see the kids."

They picked up Alissa's suitcase and rolled it toward the elevators to the parking area.

Giggling and smiling at one another, Hailey and Alissa hurried toward her car eager to get to the cottage. There was sure to be a lot of laughter.

"It's killing me that I can't introduce you to Brady and Luna before we go to the cottage," said Hailey. "But after speaking to our friend Mike Garrett, the psychologist who's been helping us handle Brady, I've decided to follow his suggestion and wait until after our time away to take you home with me. That way we avoid having me leave him twice."

Alissa placed a hand on Hailey's shoulder. "I'm disappointed too, but I understand. We need to do everything we can to help Brady with all the changes. But when I finally get to see him, he's definitely getting a hug from me."

Pleased, Hailey laughed. She knew Alissa would love both Brady and Luna.

Hailey drove into the driveway of the Seashell Cottage and announced, "Here we are."

"Wow! This is beautiful. I didn't imagine anything this luxurious. How generous of Nick."

"Let's go. I've already stocked the refrigerator and cupboards with everything I thought you'd like. Red wine, tea, fresh fruit, margarita mix, snacks and lots of lettuce, tomatoes, and strawberries from Florida."

"It all sounds delicious," Alissa said, yawning.

Hailey helped Alissa inside with her suitcase. "I'm putting you in this wing. You'll be able to see the beach when you wake up in the morning. I'm in the other wing, by the pool. Go ahead and get unpacked. I'm changing into my bathing suit. I'll meet you in the living room when you're ready. I've set aside beach towels and sunscreen, and I'll make some snacks."

Alissa gave her a hug. "Thanks for having everything so organized. After I get changed, I'll come find you."

Hailey went into her room and changed. She was happy Nick had made these arrangements. Alissa looked as tired as she felt.

In the kitchen, Hailey put together a cheese and cracker plate with fresh grapes and a few fresh strawberries. Maybe some light food would help.

After a half-hour passed and Alissa had yet to appear, Hailey crept to the door of Alissa's room and cracked it open. Alissa was lying on the bed in her bathing suit sound asleep.

Hailey's heart went out to her. She closed the door and went into the living room to pick up where she'd left off in one of the books she'd purchased for this break.

Alissa padded into the living room wearing a sheepish look. "Oh, Hailey, I'm sorry. I didn't mean to fall asleep like that."

"No worries. That's what this girls' weekend is all about— being able to do what we want when we want. I have to admit I dozed off reading my book. Some wild time we're going to have, huh?"

They laughed together. They'd always gotten along.

"How about some healthy snacks? I've got cheese, fruit, and crackers put together. And I made Nan's lemonade."

"Yum! There wasn't any food to speak of on the plane, and I think this will help settle my stomach."

"Travel isn't easy. When Nick and I went to Hawaii for our honeymoon, it was a hassle." Hailey smiled at the memory. "Not that we thought about it after we got to Maui. Since then, we've been busy. Then, with the arrival of Brady and

Luna, the only romantic time I've had lately was Valentine's Day when friends took the kids for the night."

"Yeah, pretty much the same thing with me." Alissa sighed and clasped her hands. "Paris was divine. We had such a lovely time. The food, the wine, bread, and cheese were all so delicious. Nothing like it!"

"I'm glad you got the chance to go there. In different circumstances, it would've been such fun if Nick and I could've made the trip we'd planned and met up with you for a day or two."

"Maybe next year. I still can't believe you now have two children. It happened so quickly."

"Overnight." Hailey's smile faded. "I still think of Linnie each time one of them does something cute. Luna keeps growing by leaps and bounds. I love making her smile. And her laugh is priceless."

"I'm glad you're enjoying them," said Alissa. "That's one thing Mom keeps telling me."

"I try not to worry about doing everything perfectly anymore," admitted Hailey.

"How's your new book coming along?" Alissa asked her.

Hailey felt a smile stretch across her face. "It's going to be totally adorable because it's all very real. I'm basing Charlie's reaction to his new baby sister on Brady, of course, which makes it easier than some of the other books. It's a new approach, and I'm loving it."

"I'm glad. It would be a shame to stop your work."

"Thank heavens for my babysitter. Mike recommended her to us. She's terrific. We all think the world of her. How about your situation at home?"

After learning more about what had been going on with Alissa, they decided to take a walk on the beach.

Outside, the sun was lowering in the sky. The warmth in the air was pleasant as they walked side by side.

Hailey impulsively took Alissa's arm to stop her. "Stand

right here and listen to the waves moving back and forth. Isn't that soothing?"

Alissa closed her eyes and looked up at the sky. A deep, long sigh came from her, and Hailey knew she'd been right to keep plans during this stay to a minimum. They both needed to slow down.

The frothy edges of the water swirled around their ankles. The pull of the waves as they retreated withdrew sand from around their feet, making Hailey dig her toes deeper. She'd always loved feeling a part of this timeless movement.

Arm in arm, they looked up at the seagulls above them, their white wings forming interesting shapes in the blue sky above them.

Alissa turned to her. "Thanks for arranging this. My life with Jed is amazing except for his parents. Their disapproval really hurts."

"You can't let them get to you, Alissa. They are people to be pitied," said Hailey, unable to hide her anger for the way Jed's parents acted toward Alissa and had from the first time they'd met. "If I ever meet up with them, I'll let them know."

Alissa laughed. "You're right. I can't let them get to me or Jed."

They walked on down the beach talking as fast as they could to catch up. Every once in a while, they'd stop and laugh so hard they had to hold onto their stomachs.

This, Hailey thought, was a great start to their time together.

Before they reached the cottage, a little bundle of white fur ran toward them.

"Oh, what a sweet dog," cooed Hailey, kneeling to give him a pet.

"Tiger, come back here," hollered an elderly woman slowly making her way toward them, leaning on a cane.

Hailey picked up the dog and held onto him. "I've got him."

"That pesky puppy is too much for me. I can't keep up with him," the woman said. "I'm going to have to give him away. My kids gave me a puppy for my birthday even after I asked them not to."

"You can't give him away," said Hailey. "He's adorable!"

"Will you keep him?" The woman's face softened. "He's darling and I love him, but I can't do it. It's not fair to the dog. I'm sincere. Will you take him?"

Hailey glanced at Alissa.

Tiger kissed her cheek.

"Are you serious?" asked Hailey, feeling her maternal feelings soar. "We have a dog, a dachshund, but I think Zeke would love to have a friend to play with."

"It would be a blessing if you'd take him. He's well-trained, but he's still a puppy." The woman smiled. "I have his dog dish and blanket in the car. I was on my way to the Humane Society and thought I'd give him a last run on the beach."

Aware Nick might not be as pleased as she, Hailey lifted her chin with resolve. "Okay, I'll take him."

As the woman traveled back to her car, Alissa gave Hailey a steady look. "What is Nick going to say? You already have a lot going on at your house."

Hailey set the dog down on the sand and stared into his dark eyes. Tiger looked up at her with a doggy smile and wagged his tail.

"I guess we'll find out what Nick has to say when we go home. Until then, it'll be our secret. Okay, Alissa?"

Alissa laughed. "You've loved dogs since Maddie gave you that stuffed dog years ago. Remember?"

Hailey nodded. "Oh, yes. I remember all of it." She'd been taken in once, too.

That night they shared an easy dinner of salad and garlic bread with fresh strawberries for dessert. Tiger had his dog food, enjoyed a doggie treat his former owner had given Hailey, trotted into the living room, and jumped up on the couch.

"See? He's a good dog," said Hailey.

Alissa returned her smile. "Wanna bet on where he's sleeping tonight? Not my bed, for sure."

They set their dishes in the sink and hurried into the living room.

"For tomorrow night, I've made dinner reservations at Gavin's, the gourmet restaurant at the Salty Key Inn." Hailey said, taking a seat on the couch with the dog, "But tonight, this is perfect. Movie nights are always fun. Your turn to pick which one you want to see."

"How about *Overboard*?" said Alissa.

"Great. It's one of our old standard romances. Definitely not one of Nick's favorites."

Alissa chuckled. "Chick flicks don't go very far in my house either."

Hailey pulled up the movie on the television screen and sat back on the couch, eager to see it. Moments later, the story drew her in. Though she knew how the movie ended, she loved recalling the details as she watched the movie with her sister.

Sometime later, she felt someone shaking her. "Wake up, Hailey. The movie is over." Alissa smiled down at her. "I debated whether to leave you two sleeping on the couch but thought you might be more comfortable in your bed."

Hailey sat up and rubbed her eyes. "I'm sorry ..."

"No worries," said Alissa. "The only reason I was able to stay awake was because of my nap this afternoon."

"Let's not tell anyone how lame we are," said Hailey, chuckling.

"We deserve this time," said Alissa. "It's great to be able to relax with one another. When do we ever get the chance to do something like this?

"You're right. My time is not my own anymore." *No wonder Nick and I are way behind in the baby making department,* Hailey thought. Not that she'd had time to dwell too much on it. But still, she missed their time for cuddling. When she got back home, she'd try to spice things up …

After she explained about the puppy.

EPILOGUE

A YEAR LATER...

On this April day, Hailey waited in the baggage area of the Tampa International Airport for Alissa and her family to arrive. One year ago, she and Alissa had enjoyed their girls' weekend. This time, it would be different. Alissa was bringing Jed and the kids with her.

Hailey couldn't wait to see her. Alissa had always been an inspiration to her. And with all the surprising changes in Alissa's life and hers, they had a lot to share.

Hopefully, they'd make a castle or two.

CONTINUE THE STORY

I hope you enjoyed *CHRISTMAS CASTLES*. To continue the story and find out what happens to Hailey and Alissa, you must order *CHRISTMAS STAR* by Tess Thompson, the twin book to this one.

Here are the links to *CHRISTMAS STAR:*

Nook: https://www.barnesandnoble.com/w/christmas-star-tess-thompson/1139270891

Kobo:

https://www.kobo.com/us/en/ebook/christmas-star-6

Apple: http://books.apple.com/us/book/id1563252340

Amazon: https://www.amazon.com/dp/B092HTJCWY

And if you haven't read the rest of the eleven books in the series or the anthology, here are the links to all of them: Enjoy!

1-Christmas Sisters – books2read.com/u/mdlxvw

2-Christmas Kisses – books2read.com/u/mqr75v

3-Christmas Wishes – https://books2read.com/soulsisterschristmaswishes

4-Christmas Hope – https://books2read.com/ChristmasHope

5-Christmas Dreams – https://
books2read.com/ChristmasDreamsbyEvBishop
6-Christmas Rings – https://books2read.com/u/bwdaWY
***

Christmas Stories – Anthology books2read.com/u/mZeo5B
***

7-Christmas Surprises – https://
books2read.com/soulsisterschristmassurprises
8-Christmas Yearnings – https://
books2read.com/ChristmasYearningsbyEvBishop
9-Christmas Peace – https://
books2read.com/sschristmaspeace/
10-Christmas Castles – books2read.com/u/47NVOq
11-Christmas Star – https://
books2read.com/ChristmasStarSoulSisters

ACKNOWLEDGMENTS

I wish to thank Ev Bishop, Tammy Grace, Violet Howe, and Tess Thompson for including me and my work in this group of sweet Christmas books. I met them by chance at a conference in 2019 and quickly connected with them over the idea of creating a series of short books, writing about sisters of the heart. Working on the books has been a learning experience for me because I usually write longer women's fiction, and I, like the others, have had the challenge of making the books mesh. In working together, I've grown to love these wonderful writers whom I think of as my very own soul sisters.

I hope you enjoy these stories for the holidays and all year 'round. If so, be sure and share the news with your friends. And above all, have a wonderful, joyous holiday season!

BOOKS BY JUDITH KEIM

THE HARTWELL WOMEN SERIES:

The Talking Tree – 1

Sweet Talk – 2

Straight Talk – 3

Baby Talk – 4

The Hartwell Women – Boxed Set

THE BEACH HOUSE HOTEL SERIES:

Breakfast at The Beach House Hotel – 1

Lunch at The Beach House Hotel – 2

Dinner at The Beach House Hotel – 3

Christmas at The Beach House Hotel – 4

Margaritas at The Beach House Hotel – 5

Dessert at The Beach House Hotel – 6 (2022)

THE FAT FRIDAYS GROUP:

Fat Fridays – 1

Sassy Saturdays – 2

Secret Sundays – 3

SALTY KEY INN SERIES:

Finding Me – 1

Finding My Way – 2

Finding Love – 3

Finding Family – 4

SEASHELL COTTAGE BOOKS:

A Christmas Star

Change of Heart

A Summer of Surprises

A Road Trip to Remember

The Beach Babes – (2022)

DESERT SAGE INN BOOKS:

The Desert Flowers – Rose – 1

The Desert Flowers – Lily – 2

The Desert Flowers – Willow – 3 (2022)

The Desert Flowers – Mistletoe & Holly – 4 (2022)

CHANDLER HILL INN BOOKS:

Going Home – 1

Coming Home – 2

Home at Last – 3

SOUL SISTERS AT CEDAR MOUNTAIN LODGE

Christmas Sisters – Anthology

Christmas Kisses

Christmas Castles

Christmas Stories – Soul Sisters Anthology

OTHER BOOKS

The ABC's of Living With a Dachshund

Once Upon a Friendship – Anthology

Winning BIG – a little love story for all ages

For more information: **www.judithkeim.com**

ABOUT THE AUTHOR

Judith Keim enjoyed her childhood and young-adult years in Elmira, New York, and now makes her home in Boise, Idaho, with her husband and their two dachshunds, Winston and Wally, and other members of her family.

While growing up, she was drawn to the idea of writing stories from a young age. Books were always present, being read, ready to go back to the library, or about to be discovered. All in her family shared information from the books in general conversation, giving them a wealth of knowledge and vivid imaginations.

A hybrid author who both has a publisher and self-publishes, Ms. Keim writes best-selling, heart-warming novels about women who face unexpected challenges, meet them with strength, and find love and happiness along the way. Her best-selling books are based, in part, on many of the places she's lived or visited and on the interesting people she's met, creating believable characters and realistic settings her many loyal readers love. Ms. Keim loves to hear from her readers and appreciates their enthusiasm for her stories.

"I hope you've enjoyed this book. If you have, please help other readers discover it by leaving a review on the site of your choice. And please check out my other books and series:

Hartwell Women Series

The Beach House Hotel Series

Fat Fridays Group

Salty Key Inn Series

Chandler Hill Inn Series

Seashell Cottage Books
Desert Sage Inn Series
Soul Sisters at Cedar Mountain Lodge

ALL THE BOOKS ARE NOW AVAILABLE IN AUDIO on iTunes! So fun to have these characters come alive!"

Ms. Keim can be reached at **www.judithkeim.com**

And to like her author page on Facebook and keep up with the news, go to: **http://bit.ly/2pZWDgA**

To receive notices about new books, follow her on Book Bub: **https://www.bookbub.com/authors/judith-keim**

And here's a link to where you can sign up for her periodic newsletter! http://bit.ly/2OQsb7s

She is also on Twitter @judithkeim, LinkedIn, and Goodreads. Come say hello!

Note: As part of her participation in the Soul Sisters at Cedar Mountain Lodge series, Ms. Keim is part of the Facebook Group: Soul Sisters Book Chat. To learn more about the five authors and to share friendship and fun with other readers, join here: **https://facebook.com/groups/soulsistersbookchat**